Maddie's eyes g[...]
"I've been [...]

House-hunting. Jake almost groaned aloud. Why couldn't she just stay on post where she belonged? If she moved into town, Jake would bump into her even more often than he did already.

Just yesterday he'd seen her at the offices of Children of the Day, an international Christian charity founded five years ago by Prairie Springs resident Anna Terenkov to assist innocent victims of war. He liked Anna, but lately she'd been getting on his nerves because she couldn't stop talking about her new friend Maddie. She was so sweet, Anna'd gushed. So eager to help everyone. It had been pointed out on more than one occasion that a man would have to be dead not to notice how pretty she was.

Jake definitely wasn't dead.

* * *

Homecoming Heroes: Saving children and finding love deep in the heart of Texas

Books by Brenda Coulter

Love Inspired

Finding Hope
A Family Forever
A Season of Forgiveness
At His Command

BRENDA COULTER

started writing an inspirational-romance novel the same afternoon she finished reading one for the first time. Less than a year later, she had a completed manuscript and an interested publisher. Although that first book went on to win both a HOLT Medallion and a *Romantic Times BOOKreviews* Reviewers' Choice Award, it took three rejected manuscripts before Brenda figured out what she had done right the first time. She did it again, resulting in another sale to Steeple Hill Books. That second novel was a finalist for Romance Writers of America's prestigious RITA® Award.

Married for over thirty years, Brenda and her architect husband have no pets because, after bringing up two rascally boys, they have earned a rest.

At His Command
Brenda Coulter

Steeple
Hill®

Published by Steeple Hill Books™

Special thanks and acknowledgment to
Brenda Coulter for her contribution to the
Homecoming Heroes miniseries.

STEEPLE HILL BOOKS

Steeple
Hill®

ISBN-13: 978-0-373-87496-5
ISBN-10:   0-373-87496-0

AT HIS COMMAND

Copyright © 2008 by Harlequin Books S.A.

www.SteepleHill.com

Printed in U.S.A.

You turned my wailing into dancing; you removed
my sackcloth and clothed me with joy,
that my heart may sing to you and not be silent.
O Lord my God, I will give you thanks forever.
—*Psalms* 30:11–12

With gratitude to every hero who stands ready to protect the freedoms I enjoy as an American, and with love to James E. Riley (U.S. Air Force, 1951–54), Kenneth D. Coulter (U.S. Air Force, 1947–51) and John Stokes (U.S. Marines, 1943–45; U.S. Army, 1947–49).

Chapter One

Texas attorney Jake Hopkins was severely allergic to two things: peanuts and a sweet young army nurse named Madeline Bright. Travis Wylie, Jake's law partner, took the peanut problem seriously because he'd once had to call 9-1-1 when Jake suffered a life-threatening anaphylactic reaction during dinner at an Austin restaurant. But while Travis readily acknowledged that certain women possessed a knack for turning a man every which way but loose, he steadfastly maintained that Jake couldn't be allergic to a member of his own species.

Jake knew better. There was nothing imaginary about the symptoms he suffered whenever he was in close proximity to Maddie. All he had to do was clap eyes on the chestnut-haired, blue-eyed beauty and his pulse raced, his throat closed up and his brain stalled out. Since that was pretty much what happened whenever Jake got too close to a peanut, he figured the evidence spoke for itself.

It had been four years since the sudden onset of his peanut allergy, and in that time he'd learned to give a wide berth to foods containing even a trace of the offending legumes. In the past month, he'd trained himself to be just as assiduous about avoiding Maddie.

"Madeline," he said aloud, correcting himself as he swung his black BMW convertible into the grocery-store parking lot. Using her nickname was flirting with emotional intimacy, and Jake wasn't that kind of man anymore.

Maybe he never really *had* been that kind of man. His wife had hinted at that more than a few times when she was alive. Or maybe he and Rita just hadn't been a good match to begin with. Jake had known she was dissatisfied, and sometimes he wondered if she would have gone so far as to divorce him if a freak boating accident on Lake Travis hadn't ended her life.

Poor Rita. For three years she'd clung to the stubborn belief that being married ought to temper Jake's passion for flying helicopters. She'd wanted him out of the army and out of the sky, but Jake was a second-generation West Point graduate, and a life without flying wasn't any kind of life at all.

He'd had to adjust his thinking on that after he'd awoken at a combat support hospital in the Middle East and learned he'd never walk again, let alone fly. He'd been transferred to the Army Medical Center in Landstuhl, Germany for more surgery, and a week later they'd drugged him up and loaded him on a hospital plane headed for Walter Reed Army Medical Center in Washington, D.C.

Noah Bright, his copilot-gunner and his best friend for fifteen years, had already been shipped home to Texas in a flag-draped casket.

Jake spent several weeks at Walter Reed. During that time, Rita visited twice. After she'd gone back to Texas, she drowned when a ski boat she was riding in capsized.

Jake had missed her funeral, too.

After numerous surgeries and skin grafts, Jake was finally sent home to Texas, where despite the gloomy predictions of his doctors, he learned to walk again. He wasn't terribly graceful about it, but with the help of a cane he could get around okay. Once he was, quite literally, back on his feet, his father had suggested law school.

It was a cruel irony that if Rita had lived and stuck it out with Jake, she would now have everything she'd wanted. She'd be living deep in the heart of Texas with a newly minted civilian attorney who had ruthlessly trained himself not to think about helicopters. Jake didn't even look up when one flew overhead, which was no small achievement, considering where he lived. Ensconced in the beautiful Texas Hill Country, the town of Prairie Springs hugged the east side of Fort Bonnell, the largest military installation in the United States—and home to the cavalry brigade that had trained Jake and Noah to do air combat in Apache attack helicopters.

Impatient with himself for dwelling on the past, Jake shook his head and successfully flung those depressing memories out of it. But Maddie—*Madeline*—remained.

He hated that he was having so little success fighting his insane attraction to her. He was no good for Madeline Bright, and it wasn't only because of what he'd done to Rita.

"And at five minutes before six o'clock, it's still a sweltering 102 degrees in downtown Austin," a radio announcer boomed over the end of an old Trisha Yearwood song. "I don't have to point out that that's a little warm for the third day of September."

"Then *don't* point it out," Jake muttered, irritably punching the radio's Off button and wondering what the current temperature was here in Prairie Springs, thirty miles northwest of Austin. He loved his convertible, but when he'd left home a few minutes ago he'd been compelled to close the Beemer's roof and throttle up the air conditioner.

He zipped past the handicapped parking spaces and found a spot near the end of a row. His bum leg was giving him trouble today, but the more it hurt, the more determined Jake was to walk like it didn't. The leg would never be any stronger, but Jake was convinced that pushing himself through the pain would eventually teach his nerves to quit squawking about it.

He cut the ignition, opened his door and was assailed by a blast of dry heat that reminded him of his last tour of duty in the Middle East.

As if his left leg didn't remind him of that every single day.

His right leg had caught two bullets but healed nicely; his left was a different story. Bones had been shattered and a big chunk of muscle had been blown off his thigh—and what the army surgeons had salvaged was barely enough to walk on.

Jake reached behind his seat and grabbed a cane made from the root of a sumac tree. *If you have to go, go in style,* his father had always said, so Jake collected beautifully polished natural-wood walking sticks, which he changed to suit his mood.

Maybe he should be using the black one today.

He put his left foot on the ground and swung his right leg out before pushing himself to a standing position. Sucking in a sharp breath through clenched teeth, he accepted the first lightning bolt of pain and started walking.

He'd gone just a few yards when a canary-yellow Ford Escape peeled around the corner and slid into an empty parking space just ahead of him. The door was immediately flung open and a pair of trim, tanned female legs emerged.

Pretty. They reminded him of—

His heart skipped a beat when he saw the rest of the woman. Sure enough, it was Madeline Bright. Jake froze, hoping she hadn't noticed him.

She hadn't. She closed her door and made for the store entrance with her usual energetic stride.

Lost in admiration, Jake followed her with his eyes. She was all army—capable and confident and strong as iron— but she was still every inch a lady. She was fine-boned and tenderhearted and vulnerable in the most appealing ways. From the subtly swinging curves of her dark, shoulder-length hair, which she wore pulled back and above her collar when in uniform, to her slim pink toes, which Jake had glimpsed when she wore sandals, she was lovely.

She was probably the only woman in the world who could make a bulky Army Combat Uniform look good, but Jake much preferred the way she was dressed today. She wore sand-colored cargo shorts, a white tank top that set off her tan, a yellow-patterned scarf in her hair and large sunglasses that made her look like someone the paparazzi ought to be chasing.

Forgetting for a moment that she was his number-two allergen, Jake imagined pulling her onto his good knee and kissing her breathless. Then reason returned and advised him to beat a retreat to his car before Maddie happened to glance over her shoulder.

It wasn't that she wouldn't be delighted to see him. Whenever they met, her blue eyes widened with pleasure and her bow-shaped mouth curved into a welcoming smile. As a kid, she'd had an obvious crush on Jake, her much older brother's best friend. It had been cute back then, but now she was an eminently desirable woman whom Jake had no business desiring, and that made her interest in him a very dangerous thing.

In the month since her arrival in Prairie Springs, Jake hadn't been able to go anywhere without running into her or hearing people talk about her, and he was beginning to resent it. The whole world was Madeline Bright's oyster; couldn't she leave this one little Texas town to *him?*

Behind him, a car horn blared, reminding him that he was standing in the middle of the traffic lane. Afraid that the noise would prompt Maddie to turn around, he impulsively made for a rusted-out pickup truck. His half-formed thought was to lurk behind the truck's cab until Maddie was safely inside the store. But his bum leg chose that instant to give out and he pitched forward. Letting go of his cane, he broke his fall with his hands.

Pain shot up his left leg as though a mad pianist was playing glissandos on his raw nerves. As the pavement seared his belly through his shirt, Jake closed his eyes and forced himself to draw slow, deep breaths. It was another second or two before he realized the deafening noise assaulting his ears was no pain-induced hallucination; he'd triggered the car alarm of the red Camry next to the truck.

Oh, this just kept getting better and better. But at least he was safe from Maddie.

"Jake?"

At the sound of her voice, Jake groaned and squeezed his eyes more tightly shut. Better and better and better.

"Jake! Please tell me you're all right!"

He was aware that she crouched beside him, but he still

flinched when she touched his shoulder. "Give me a minute," he growled.

"Everything's going to be all right," she promised, pitching her voice to be heard over the Camry's alarm. She stroked the back of Jake's head, multiplying his misery with her gentle touch. "Just tell me where it hurts."

His eyes popped open. If he didn't quickly convince her that he was perfectly fine, she'd be running her hands all over his body, checking for broken bones.

"Madeline." He rolled over and sat up smartly. He considered smiling, but with his teeth clenched against the pain, he figured he'd look maniacal, rather than reassuring. "What a surprise."

She was clearly in no mood for chitchat. "Where are you hurt?"

"Just jarred the leg, that's all." They were still shouting at each other. "Could you hand me my stick?"

She hesitated, sweeping him with a doubtful look, but then she went to retrieve his cane. While she was gone, Jake flattened one palm against the scalding door of the pickup and one against the blistering fender of the Camry and hauled himself up.

When Maddie returned, the grim set of her mouth communicated her displeasure that he'd risen without assistance. "Jake, you should have let me—"

"I'm fine," he interrupted, reaching for the cane. "Thanks."

She looked him up and down, skepticism written all over her pretty face. "Where did you get hit? All I saw was the car speeding away, and then I noticed a pair of legs sticking out from behind this truck."

"The car didn't hit me," Jake said.

"Well, praise God for that." Maddie's relief was obvious as she removed her sunglasses and hooked them on the neck band of her shirt. "But what happened?"

Dilemma. Should he admit the truth, that he'd dived behind the truck to avoid being seen by the woman who'd been starring in his dreams for the past month? Or should he attempt to salvage his pride with a little white lie?

Easy call. "I tripped. Over…something," he mumbled.

She leaned toward him and cupped a hand to her ear. "Pardon?"

"I tripped over something," Jake repeated loudly, just as the car alarm ceased its obnoxious honking. The lie hadn't been a good one to begin with, and yelling it into the sudden silence didn't improve it any.

Confusion wrinkled Maddie's forehead as her gaze roamed over the smooth asphalt of the perfectly level parking lot. There wasn't a crack, a bump or even a pebble to be seen. She looked back at Jake and frowned. "Your face is flushed."

Great. Now he was blushing like a teenager. He jerked his gaze away from her dangerously beautiful eyes, which were as deep and blue as the sea of bluebonnets that covered the central Texas hills in springtime. "The heat's getting to me, that's all."

She stepped closer and laid her palm against the side of his face, no doubt checking his temperature. "Are you staying hydrated?"

"Yeah." Jake shied away from her touch, hoping she hadn't noticed his racing pulse.

He'd never felt more ridiculous in his life. He was a thirty-nine-year-old combat veteran, a former U.S. Army aviator who'd flown Apache attack helicopters and twice been decorated for valor. So why was it that whenever this sweet young woman appeared on his radar screen, his heart sped up and he trembled like a nervous Chihuahua?

Maddie brushed some fine gravel off the front of his damp shirt. "I worry about you, Jake."

Well, that was just great. All he'd needed was one more thing to feel guilty about where she was concerned.

"Is he okay?" A plump, elderly woman holding a paper bag of groceries in one arm approached the driver's door of the Camry. She looked anxiously from Maddie to Jake, who was now leaning heavily on his cane and wishing he'd just called for a pizza instead of coming to the store in search of dinner.

"Yes, ma'am," Maddie said sweetly. "He'll be fine."

"Oh, good. I saw him fall, but my old legs don't move very fast." The woman shook her head. "Wasn't it just the oddest thing, the way he took that flying leap and—"

"I'm fine," Jake interrupted. The less said about his flying leap, the better. "I appreciate your concern, ma'am, and I'm sorry I triggered your alarm."

She dismissed that with an airy wave of her hand. "Isn't it annoying, the way those dumb things go off every time somebody breathes wrong?" As Jake shifted out of her way, she opened the Camry's door. "If I wanted to steal a car, I'd set off the alarm first to make sure nobody paid any attention to me." Cackling at her own joke, she got in and closed the door.

Maddie slid a protective arm around Jake's waist and silently urged him to back up a little more. Nurse or not, she was a natural-born caregiver. But Jake didn't want to be fussed over by anyone, least of all by Noah's kid sister.

Noah.

The memory of their last hour together was never far from Jake's mind. How could it be, after what he had done? For more than five years the guilt had gnawed at his insides, ensuring he never forgot how his mistake had cost Noah his life.

"Where's your car?" Maddie asked with brisk purpose, almost as though she meant to hoist Jake over her shoulder and carry him there.

He shook his head. "I'm going to the store."

"No," she said firmly. "Whatever you need, I'll get it. You took a bad spill, and you're going home to rest that leg. Now where's your car?"

Giving in, he pointed with his stick and then hobbled in that direction, each step on his left leg pure agony. Since he used the cane on his right side, Maddie grasped his left arm and stuck to him as though she'd been glued there. She wasn't supporting any of his weight, but it was clear she was ready to do so if called upon.

"You need water," she announced as Jake collapsed onto the driver's seat of the Beemer and stashed his cane behind it. "Wait here. I have some in my car."

"No need." Jake reached for the quart-size bottle of spring water on his passenger seat. After removing the cap, he offered the first drink to Maddie.

She grinned down at him and shook her head. "Still quite the gentleman, aren't you, Captain Hopkins?"

"Don't call me that." In the past five years, he'd done his best to forget his old life. He wished the rest of the world would forget it, too.

He saluted Maddie with the bottle and took a long pull of sun-warmed water.

"Good." She gave his shoulder an approving pat. "Now get some air going."

Jake started his engine and switched the air conditioner to its highest setting. "Happy now?"

Maddie shook her head. "I can see the pain in your eyes, Jake." She reached out to touch his face, then apparently thought better of it, which was a very good thing. "Do you have your meds with you?"

"No." He had a prescription, naturally, but he refused to eat painkillers like candy, so most of the time he just gritted his teeth and bore it. At the moment, however, drugs sounded pretty good.

"Anna Terenkov told me you live in an apartment over your law offices," Maddie said.

Jake nodded, wondering what else their mutual friend had said about him. Maddie—*Madeline*—knew him far too well already.

"I think you're okay to drive that short a distance," she said. "It can't be more than a mile from here. Just promise you'll go straight home."

"I will." Anything to get rid of her.

"Thank you." She leaned down and kissed his cheek. It happened so fast, Jake didn't have time to avoid it. Fortunately he didn't have time to *enjoy* it, either.

"It's unbelievably hot out here," Maddie said cheerfully as she tucked an escaped lock of hair under the yellow scarf she wore as a headband.

She had always been crazy about yellow and still wore at least a touch of it whenever she could. It was the color of the sun, she'd told Jake years ago. The color of happiness.

"What am I getting you from the store?" she asked.

"Nothing." He didn't want her doing him any favors. "You don't have time to—"

"Actually, I do, because this is my day off. And guess what?" Her eyes glowed with happiness. "I've been house hunting."

House hunting? Jake almost groaned aloud. Why couldn't she just stay on post, where she belonged? If she moved into town, Jake would bump into her even more often than he did already.

Just yesterday, he'd seen her at the offices of Children of the Day, an international Christian charity founded five years ago by Prairie Springs resident Anna Terenkov to assist innocent victims of war. For the past year, Jake had been doing pro bono legal work for the organization, so he'd become friendly with Anna and with Olga, her delightfully outlandish mother.

He genuinely liked both women, but lately Anna and Olga had been getting on his nerves because they couldn't stop talking about their new friend Maddie. She was so sweet, they gushed. So eager to help everyone. And Olga, the inveterate matchmaker, had pointed out on more than one occasion that a man would have to be dead not to notice how pretty she was.

Jake definitely wasn't dead.

Dreamy-eyed, Maddie stared over the Beemer's roof. "I'm looking for a place where I can have a flower garden and a kitchen big enough to actually cook in." Her gaze shifted back to Jake. "The kitchenettes in the bachelor officers quarters at Fort Bonnell must be some architect's idea of a joke, and…" She stopped and gave herself a little shake. "Never mind. What am I getting you from the store?"

"Nothing, thanks. I wanted something for dinner, but I'll

just go home and make a sandwich." With two stale pieces of bread—all that was left of the loaf were the heels—and the last thin sliver of ham, which he'd have to sniff carefully before he risked eating. He never went grocery shopping until he was completely out of food.

"Tell you what," she said brightly. Maddie—*Madeline*—was always as cheerful as a songbird. "I'll cook something for you."

"No." Panic roared through Jake. But he realized he'd spoken too sharply, so he added, "Thanks, but I have to finish some paperwork tonight."

"Don't worry. I'll fix something quick and easy."

Jake opened his mouth on another protest and felt it die in his throat. How could he decline such a generous offer without stomping all over her feelings? "All right," he said unhappily. "Thank you."

"Don't look so delighted." Gazing at him with amused affection, she ruffled his hair. "You can work until dinner's ready, and as soon as we've eaten, you can go right back to your papers. It's not like this will be a date or anything."

No, it would certainly not be a date or anything. Not with her. Jake would give up women entirely before he'd make a mistake of that magnitude.

Her expression turned wistful. "It's been a long time since we shared a meal."

At those words, memories Jake had been fleeing for years caught up to him and swirled around him like the rising waters of a flash flood. During his and Noah's second year at West Point, they'd spent the first few days of their Christmas leave at Noah's home in Dallas. Jake had liked Noah's mother and his happy, bouncy little sister, who must have been six or seven at the time. Maddie and her mama had more or less adopted Jake, and he'd seen them often in the years that followed. But in those dark days when Jake had lain in the hospital broken in body and spirit, his faith failing as guilt consumed him, he had refused their visits.

Since that time he'd had no contact with the Brights. Then last month Maddie had appeared, all grown up and exquisitely lovely, right here in Prairie Springs. She'd been openly delighted to see Jake, who was still resolved to stay out of her life. The problem was that whenever this grown-up Maddie smiled, every molecule in Jake's body shifted toward her, as though she was the moon and he was an ocean tide.

Defeated, he opened his wallet and handed her some grocery money.

"What sounds good to you?" she asked.

She sounded good to him. Her melodious drawl made him think of warm honey dripping from a spoon. His gaze strayed to her mouth and he wondered what it would be like to—

"Jake?"

He hastily collected his wandering wits. "Maybe some kind of pasta. And I like salad. But you should know I've developed a severe allergy to peanuts." *And you,* he added silently. Just look what she was doing to his brain at this very moment.

Her fine dark eyebrows drew together. "Peanuts?"

"Yeah. I had my first reaction about four years ago. I guess it happens that way sometimes."

"Do you carry—"

"Epinephrine." He patted the right front pocket of his jeans. Since that horrifying episode at the restaurant in Austin, he'd never been without his emergency lifesaving kit.

Maddie nodded. "I'll be careful to read the labels on

everything I buy." She stepped back and started to close his car door, then hesitated. "What about dessert? Do you still like sweet things?"

Sweet things? "Oh, yeah," he breathed, trying not to stare at her mouth. Her rosy pink lips looked natural, but she might have been wearing lipstick. "I'm a sugar fiend. Cookies, cakes, pies, ice cream…"

"Ice cream." Her smile blossomed. "Jake Hopkins, you're a man after my own heart."

He managed a weak smile to hide his terror.

Chapter Two

As endless waves of oppressive heat shimmered up from the parking lot's surface, Maddie bit the insides of her checks and watched Jake drive away. Something was troubling him, and she was determined to get to the bottom of it.

He was no longer the brash, swaggering helicopter pilot she'd sighed over as a girl, but she admired the man he'd become. Jake had pulled himself together and risen like a phoenix from the ashes of his grief. He had learned to walk again. He'd gone to law school. And while he didn't appear to be attending church anymore, he was supporting an eminently worthwhile Christian charity; according to their mutual friend, Anna Terenkov, Jake made substantial gifts of his time and legal expertise to Children of the Day.

He looked dearly familiar, yet he had changed. Time had softened the sharp angles of his jaw and filled out his tall, lean-as-a-whippet frame. His dark, straight hair, which he still wore in a traditional cut parted on the side, was now shot with silver, and his brown eyes crinkled at the corners when he smiled. His mouth seemed firmer and thinner than

Maddie remembered, but it hinted at a determination she liked. He was more handsome than ever, she concluded as she turned back toward the grocery store entrance.

He intrigued her on every level, but she was beginning to despair that he would never stop thinking of her as Noah's baby sister and see the woman she'd become. She had never flirted so hard in her life, or to so little effect.

She claimed a shopping cart and pushed it toward a pair of automatic doors. As they swung open, delivering a welcome blast of chilly air, Maddie squared her shoulders and resolved not to give up on Jake. He might be uninterested in romance, but he still needed a friend, and friendship just happened to be Maddie's specialty.

She tossed a cheery wave to a new acquaintance behind one of the cash registers, then made a beeline for the produce department. After a year's deployment to a place where she couldn't always count on having a banana to slice over her breakfast cereal, being able to buy all the fresh produce she wanted was true luxury. She halted beside a display of golden pineapples and selected one that seemed heavy for its size.

That means it's full of juice.

As Maddie heard the voice of Whitney Paterson Harpswell in her head, a pain zinged through her chest. It just didn't seem possible that her best friend might never come home.

They'd grown up together in Dallas. Whitney had joined the army, too, but had gone into a different field, so she and Maddie now did most of their confiding via e-mail. Whitney had recently married fellow soldier John Harpswell, and their unit had subsequently deployed to the Middle East. The day after Maddie's arrival in Prairie Springs, she'd heard the devastating news that Whitney and John had been missing for more than a month.

Since then, Maddie had been fighting to hold on to hope.

She sighed heavily and moved to the lettuce counter to select salad greens for Jake's dinner.

Jake. She couldn't recall the last time they'd had dinner together, but she clearly remembered the *first* time. She'd been a lisping first-grader when Noah had brought one of his fellow West Point cadets home for Christmas.

Maddie had fallen instantly in love. She'd dreamed about Jake until her sophomore year of high school, when she finally began to notice boys her own age. But even after her childish crush had run its course, she'd kept a special place in her heart just for Jake, and he continued to be a powerful influence in her life. It was Jake who encouraged her to pursue her dream of becoming a nurse. Later, after he expressed his profound admiration for the doctors and nurses at the combat support hospitals overseas, Maddie had joined the army in hopes of becoming one of those heroes.

That had turned out to be a mistake. While she was proud of her affiliation with the U.S Army Nurse Corps, she wasn't cut out for nursing soldiers and civilians in a war zone. The horrors she'd witnessed during her deployment had nearly crushed her naturally sunny spirit.

As she slipped a bunch of green onions into a plastic bag, she recalled the day she'd e-mailed Whitney and confessed that she was terrified of losing herself. Every time she watched a boy-soldier die and every time she saw a child who had been maimed by an insurgent's bomb, another piece of Madeline Bright disintegrated.

"You've done a wonderful service to our country,"

Whitney had written back. "But maybe your personality isn't suited to ER and trauma nursing. Wouldn't you rather take care of pregnant women and newborn babies, or something like that?"

Yes, she would. So as her tour had drawn to a close, Maddie had collected the necessary recommendations and applied for admission to a new obstetrics program at the Fort Bonnell/Prairie Springs Medical Center. A couple of months of distance-learning classes on her computer, plus some on-the-job training with a nurse preceptor, all overseen by the hospital's head nurse and the supervisor of the OB floor, and Maddie would be living a whole new life. Nursing happy expectant mothers was exactly what she wanted now.

That and a little house with a flower garden and maybe even a dog.

She had no idea how long a convalescence her injured heart would require, but until she could process and put away the disturbing memories of the past year and recover her old sunny spirit, she would continue faking it. She hated deception, but her friends and loved ones had always depended on her to be upbeat. And surely she wouldn't have to pretend for long before she became her old cheerful self again.

Reminding herself that Jake was waiting, she pushed her worries aside and quickly finished her shopping.

The law offices of Hopkins and Wylie were just three blocks from the green space at the center of town. Maddie had never been inside the graceful white house, a lone example of Greek Revival architecture in a neighborhood of Victorians, but she'd marked its location after Anna Terenkov had pointed it out one day.

She parked on the street. Leaving her own sack of groceries in the car, she hefted Jake's and started up his front walk, which led her past a massive crape myrtle thrusting its exuberant purple blossoms skyward. Looking higher, she scanned the long, green-shuttered windows of the house's second story. According to Anna, Jake had knocked down most of the interior walls on that floor and converted the space to a beautiful loft apartment.

Maddie climbed the steps between four stately white columns, noting with approval the flagstaffs jutting from the two innermost columns. In the hot, dry breeze, the Stars and Stripes and Texas's Lone Star flag snapped softly behind her as she shifted the grocery bag to her left hip and pressed the intercom button beside the door.

"Is that you, Madeline?" Jake's voice floated out of the little brass grille.

She couldn't resist teasing him. "Were you expecting the pizza delivery boy?"

"Not hardly," he drawled. "You promised me a home-cooked meal." A buzz followed by a metallic *thunk* told her he'd just remotely disengaged the door's lock. "I'll meet you at the top of the stairs."

She stepped into a spacious foyer redolent of old leather and lemon furniture oil. A polished reception desk presided over a semicircle of wing chairs and a few small tables holding brass lamps, all resting on the biggest oriental rug Maddie had ever seen. The furniture appeared well used, but very good; according to Anna, the pieces were castoffs from the family home of Jake's partner, whose father owned one of the largest cattle ranches in Texas.

The focal point of the large space was a gracefully curved

oak staircase. It was truly a thing of beauty, but the room's tall ceiling made it a long climb to the second floor.

"Jake, I hate to think of you negotiating all these stairs," Maddie called as she tripped lightly up them.

"I don't." He appeared at the top landing, leaning on his cane. "There's an elevator at the back of the house. All we had to do was enlarge the hole for the old dumb waiter in the kitchen."

As Maddie reached his side, he extended his free arm for the groceries. It was a gentlemanly move, but Maddie was army-strong and Jake had enough work to do simply keeping both legs under him, so she shook her head and assured him the bag wasn't heavy. He nodded briefly, accepting that.

His hair was wet, and he smelled of the same outdoorsy soap Noah had favored. He'd changed into black running shorts and a burnt-orange Texas Longhorns T-shirt.

Unable to contain her curiosity, Maddie looked down. Beginning at Jake's knee and disappearing under the hem of his shorts, angry pink scars covered his misshapen left thigh.

"Sorry." One corner of his mouth lifted in a self-deprecating smile. "My leg was feeling tender, and sometimes shorts are more comfortable than jeans."

He could hardly imagine that a nurse would be shocked by his scars, so Maddie assumed he was apologizing for his casual attire and bare feet. "I'm wearing shorts, too," she pointed out.

"Yeah, I noticed." His voice sounded pinched. Maddie figured it was because his leg hurt.

He couldn't seem to hold her gaze for more than a second or two before his dark eyes shifted away. Maddie ascribed that to the pain, too, because Jake couldn't possibly be nervous in the company of someone he'd known since she was a child.

But *she* was nervous, and to cover that up, she indicated the brass umbrella stand next to her. It appeared to hold at least a dozen walking sticks. "You sure do have a lot of these things."

Jake braced his feet and held up the cane he'd been leaning on. "This handle's carved from olive wood. Look at the grain."

Maddie skimmed her fingertips over the honey-colored swirls in the smooth wood, which was still warm from Jake's grasp. "It's beautiful."

He nodded. "My first cane was one of those clunky aluminum-and-rubber things. The day Dad saw it, he went out and bought a cypress stick with a brass handle. He challenged me to find a cane more beautiful than the one he'd discovered, and it became something of a competition between us." Jake returned the cane's tip to the floor and shifted his weight to his stronger leg. "I think it was his way of helping me come to terms with the fact that while I've come a long way, I'll never walk without help."

Knowing Jake wouldn't appreciate the compassionate tears that had begun to gather in her eyes, Maddie turned away from him and surveyed his apartment.

The sparsely furnished loft featured glowing maple floors and worn but still beautiful oriental rugs. Between the long bare windows, the white walls were hung with oil paintings, most of them Texas Hill Country landscapes.

"Who did all of these?" Maddie wondered aloud.

"Mama. She took up painting after we lost Dad."

"Your dad?" Shocked, Maddie turned to look at him. "When?"

Jake's gaze dropped like a stone, hiding his irises behind thick, dark lashes. "Almost two years ago."

"Oh, Jake, I'm sorry."

Noah had known Connor Hopkins, a district attorney, quite well. Both he and Jake had always spoken of the man with the utmost admiration. But Maddie and her mama hadn't met either of Jake's parents until Noah's funeral. On that day Maddie had been too upset to converse with Connor and Alma Jean, although she'd been gratified to know they were deeply affected by Noah's death.

The families met again at Rita's funeral, and when Jake was finally brought home to Texas, they met a few more times at the hospital, where Jake continued to refuse all visitors except his parents. In the year that followed, Maddie's mother and Jake's exchanged occasional phone calls. But soon after Jake entered law school, they'd lost touch.

Thinking of all Jake had endured—losing his career, his ability to walk, his best friend, his wife and his father—made Maddie's heart ache. She knew it wasn't right to question God, but why had Jake been made to suffer so much in so short a time?

Maddie opened her mouth to speak, but no words came out, so she cleared her throat and tried again. "How's your mother doing?"

"She misses him something fierce."

As did Jake, judging by his bowed shoulders and the quiet intensity of his words. But as much as she pitied him, Maddie was glad they were finally communicating on something other than a superficial level. In the past month Jake had shied away from discussing any subject that might be construed as remotely personal, which made no sense, given their history. He wouldn't even talk to her about Noah.

She moved closer and put her hand on his shoulder. It was a gesture of sympathy, nothing more, but he stiffened at her touch, so she withdrew. She covered her embarrassment by walking across the room to admire one of the paintings.

She loved bluebonnets, and here were endless, undulating drifts of them under a broad sky dotted with cotton-ball clouds. A well-traveled dirt road ran up the middle of the picture and past a bunch of scrubby cedar trees before disappearing over a hill, making Maddie wonder what lay on the other side.

She heard the muffled thuds of Jake's cane and footsteps on the carpet behind her and was just about to turn when something brushed against her bare leg. Startled, she looked down and saw a large orange cat with ugly brown and black splotches arching against her. When the animal raised its head, she noticed its eyes were crossed. It was also missing a hind leg.

"Meet Tripod," Jake said.

"Oh, the poor thing." Maddie shifted the grocery bag to her hip and stooped to pet the unfortunate cat. "I never knew you were a cat person, Jake."

"I'm not. Travis, my partner, found him on the back doorstep one morning. When we learned our office manager had been feeding him, Travis bought a litter box and invited him to move in. I objected on the grounds that a law office is no place for pets. But Travis presented a convincing argument that nobody could possibly hate a pair of attorneys who provided a home for an ugly, crippled cat."

Maddie chuckled as she scratched behind Tripod's ears.

"I hate to tell you, Jake, but there are actually people in this world who don't like lawyers *or* cats."

She looked up in time to see him surrender a brief smile, but the humor that lit his brown eyes faded quickly and he averted his gaze. Maddie wanted to shake him and demand to know why he found it so impossible to look at her for more than two seconds at a time.

Sighing inwardly, she smoothed the fur on Tripod's head with her cupped hand. The cat held still, bearing her attentions with a distinctly uncatlike patience, and Maddie couldn't help comparing his behavior to that of his master. Jake could give lessons in aloofness to even the most catlike of cats.

He shifted his weight, unconsciously drawing Maddie's attention to his scars, which were now at eye level. Considering the extent of the damage to his leg, she could only marvel at the courage and determination it must have taken for Jake to learn to walk again.

He noticed the direction of her gaze. "It's a mess, isn't it?"

She nodded slowly, then gave Tripod one last caress and stood up. "But God was merciful. You didn't lose the leg, and you learned to walk again."

"Merciful?" Jake's mouth twisted as though the word tasted bad. "Your brother died, Madeline. Excuse me if I don't see anything 'merciful' about what happened that night."

His belligerent tone and the harsh light in his eyes shocked her, but she reminded herself that a world of pain lay behind them. And this was actually a breakthrough, because it was the first time Jake had mentioned Noah. In the past month Maddie had tried several times to bring her brother into their conversations, but Jake had always been quick to change the subject. It was abundantly clear that he had never accepted Noah's death.

Maddie sent up a silent, urgent prayer that God would give her the words Jake most needed to hear.

"It still hurts when I think about Noah," she began carefully. "But I don't wish him back here, Jake, because he's with God." She hesitated. "You believe that, don't you?"

A muscle twitched in his jaw as his anger faded to a bleak acceptance that tore at Maddie's heart. "That's what I was taught," he said quietly. "But why would a loving God allow—" He broke off and shook his head, looking weary and defeated as he stared at a patch of fading sunlight that had fallen across the richly patterned rug. "I just don't know anymore."

Maddie was moved to comfort him with a friendly touch, but she checked the impulse. "Have you ever read the first chapter of Romans?"

"Yeah, sure. A long time ago. But that's not relevant in today's—"

"But it *is*," she interrupted eagerly. "Nothing could be *more* relevant, Jake. That chapter says we all know in our hearts that God is real. You're just tired and confused, Jake, that's all. The truth is right there in your heart. You just need to be still and let God—"

"Madeline." He looked pointedly at his watch. "I'm sorry, but as I said earlier, I have to work tonight."

"I forgot." Embarrassment burned her cheeks as she emitted a nervous little laugh. "I'm sorry for preaching at you. I promised to make you a quick dinner and then get out of here, didn't I?"

He nodded. "The kitchen's this way."

She followed him into an attractive if somewhat sterile-looking room with bare windows, stainless-steel appliances and empty black-marble countertops.

"I'm not a cook," Jake said, "but I do have pots and pans and things." He made a vague, helpless gesture. "Somewhere."

Hiding a smile, Maddie set her groceries on the counter. When she began unloading her purchases, Jake turned to go. Thinking he might stay for another minute if she said something clever, she racked her brain for a good conversation opener. By the time he reached the doorway, she was desperate and simply blurted, "I like it that you're not ashamed to be seen in shorts."

He turned, his dark eyebrows raised in surprise. "I do my best to avoid scaring small children," he said dryly. "But otherwise, I don't give it much thought."

Maddie couldn't think of a response to that, but as he again turned away, another string of foolish words slid out of her mouth. "I also like that you don't try to hide your gray hair."

This time when he looked at her, amusement danced in his eyes. Encouraged, Maddie folded her arms and pretended to study him critically. "You're a very handsome man, you know."

Jake snorted. "For an old guy and a gimp?"

"Absolutely." Maddie flashed a saucy grin. "If I'm not careful, I might fall in love with you."

His smile flattened. "Then see that you *are* careful, Madeline. For both our sakes." He continued to hold her gaze for a moment, his dark eyes unfathomable, and then he walked away.

"Not too bright, Bright," Maddie berated herself in a whisper as she pulled a small carton of ice cream out of the bag and stowed it in Jake's empty freezer. How did she always manage to say exactly the wrong thing to him?

In the old days Jake had been easy to talk to. But now it seemed Maddie couldn't open her mouth without tripping a conversational land mine. Had he really changed that much?

She spotted a CD player next to Jake's coffeepot and switched it on. As country music filled the kitchen, Maddie realized there were at least two things about Jake that hadn't changed: he still wore those burnt-orange Texas Longhorn T-shirts and he still listened to George Strait.

Humming along as George sang, Maddie located a large pot and filled it with water for her pasta. As she began putting together a simple tomato-based sauce, her mind wandered over the events leading up to that day last month when she'd seen Jake for the first time in more than five years.

She hadn't returned from the Middle East on a regular troop transport. Instead, she'd boarded a C-17 hospital plane to accompany a sick, frightened five-year-old boy to Texas.

The child of a deceased American soldier and a foreign national, Ali Tabiz Willis had suffered an injury to his heart in the same bomb blast that killed his mother. Maddie had helped Dr. Mike Montgomery care for the orphaned boy at their combat support hospital, and she'd been standing beside Dr. Mike when he'd placed an overseas call to his friends at Children of the Day and begged for their help in saving little Ali's life.

Children of the Day had swung into action and lined up a pediatric cardiac surgeon to perform the highly specialized heart surgery in Austin. They also discovered that the boy's paternal grandfather was none other than retired army general Marlon Willis of Prairie Springs, Texas. The general hadn't even known that his estranged son had fathered a child.

Maddie had no idea how many people had ultimately

been involved in getting Ali to Fort Bonnell, but she knew strings had been pulled, red tape cut and favors called in. Even then, there had been some tricky legal issues to untangle, and that was where Jake had come in.

Maddie smiled to herself as she washed salad greens. Maybe Jake wasn't sure he believed in God anymore, but God had certainly used him to accomplish His plan for Ali Willis.

After their long trip to Texas, Maddie had stuck by the little orphan's side until she'd seen him comfortably settled in his room at the Fort Bonnell/Prairie Springs Medical Center. He had just been introduced to his grandfather, so Maddie waited until the uncertainty had disappeared from his sweet dark eyes and he was chatting comfortably with the general before kissing his velvety cheek and taking her leave.

Intent on finding a hot shower and a soft bed, Maddie had charged toward an opening elevator door, nearly mowing down a man with a cane who was attempting to exit. With a profuse apology on the tip of her tongue, she stepped back and looked up into a pair of startled brown eyes and wondered for an instant if she was already asleep and dreaming.

"Jake?"

"Hello, Maddie."

He was smiling, but there was something guarded in his expression that kept her from throwing her arms around his neck. He hadn't reached for *her,* either, so she wondered if he was feeling guilty about refusing her visits at the hospital all those years ago. He'd been shocked and grieving and in pain; she had understood that, so there was nothing to forgive.

"Somebody mentioned an army nurse named Maddie Bright," he said as he stepped away from the elevator. "But I didn't think they could be talking about *you.*"

"I finished nursing school and joined the army," she blurted, then felt stupid for stating something so obvious.

A corner of Jake's mouth quirked in amusement as his gaze traveled slowly down to her boots. "I can see that, Lieutenant."

Maddie was suddenly self-conscious. This was their first meeting in years, and here she stood in baggy, wrinkled fatigues and clunky boots. She hadn't showered since yesterday, and it had been months since her mouth had been anywhere near a tube of lipstick. Even worse, she'd sucked her last breath mint somewhere over the Atlantic.

She quickly decided that none of those things mattered. She'd have crawled through slime for this chance to see Jake and satisfy herself that he was all right.

"Mama and I were overjoyed when we heard you'd learned to walk again," she said. "And when you started law school…oh, Jake, we were so proud." Her voice cracked on that last word and her eyes had teared up, so she emitted a self-conscious little laugh. "Sorry. I'm exhausted."

"Is your mother well?" Once again, Maddie detected an odd wariness in his expression.

"She's fine." Maddie grasped a lock of loose hair that had flopped against her cheek and tucked it behind her ear. "She's still with the accounting firm, but she's on a business trip right now, so it'll be a few days before I head up to Dallas to see her."

Jake's broad shoulders dropped a little and he appeared to relax. "Please give her my best."

"I will. I can't wait to tell her I bumped into you. But what are you *doing* here?"

"Practicing law. My partner and I hung out a shingle in

Prairie Springs just over a year ago." He paused. "I've been representing General Willis in the matter of his grandson."

"Ali? Oh, Jake this is wonderful!" Maddie knew she was grinning like a goof, but at the moment she was happier than she'd been in years. "I guess you're the attorney everyone's been talking about."

His answering smile was wistful and brief. "The general asked me to stop by, and I don't know how long he's planning to be here at the hospital, so I'd better get in there."

Maddie was reluctant to see him go, but she inclined her head. Since he was living and working right here in Prairie Springs, she'd have ample opportunities to see him.

"All grown up," he murmured, shaking his head as though he could hardly believe it. "You look good, Maddie."

She made a wry face. "Jake, I'm fresh off a plane from the Middle East. Although 'fresh' probably isn't the best word choice. As I'm sure you remember, it's a very long, noisy, uncomfortable trip in a C-17."

Those words had proved to be conversation killers. They'd chased the warmth from Jake's eyes and made his mouth tighten. "I remember," he'd said, and then he'd mumbled something about the two of them having a long talk later.

Maddie was still waiting for that long talk. They'd come close to having it just a little while ago, but Jake had clammed up again.

Maddie dropped some sweet Italian sausage into a skillet to brown. She hoped Jake liked sausage, because if the way to a man's heart really *was* through his stomach, maybe he'd relax over dinner and they'd finally have that talk.

Her conscience pricked her, but she ignored it. She had

assured Jake this wouldn't be like a date, but that was exactly what she was hoping it would turn out to be.

Seated in his leather recliner with his feet elevated and a stack of folders on the lamp table beside him, Jake silently acknowledged that he was a low-down skunk. No woman deserved to be treated the way he'd been treating Maddie.

His totally inappropriate attraction was *his* problem, not hers. She was just trying to be friendly and helpful. That was the way she was, the way she had always been. That was why she'd gazed respectfully at his mama's awful paintings and petted his nuisance of a cat. And that was why she hadn't told him off and stormed out of his apartment after she'd made that innocent joke about falling in love and he'd made her feel like a fool.

He wished he could take it all back and tell her…

Tell her *what,* exactly?

"She's not for you, Hopkins," he muttered under his breath.

Tripod leaped onto the chair and settled across Jake's right thigh, as always avoiding his weak leg by some strange instinct. When Jake absently laid his hand on the cat's long back and stroked a couple of times, Tripod began to purr.

"Glad one of us is happy," Jake groused, tossing aside the contract he'd been pretending to read. He wasn't going to get any work done with Maddie in his kitchen sautéeing onions—he could smell them—and singing along with one of his favorite CDs.

She had as pure and perfect an alto as he had ever heard, and she was going to be the death of him. Jake cocked his head and listened more closely, impressed that she knew all of the words to "I Cross My Heart," a song George Strait had ridden to the top of the country charts a few years ago. As she sang about true love and lifelong devotion, Jake stared hopelessly at the whirling paddles of the ceiling fan above him.

If Madeline Bright had been put on earth with strict instructions to torture him, she couldn't possibly be doing a better job than she was doing right now.

He wished she would just hurry up and go away. He wished it so hard that he was almost tempted to pray for it.

Which just went to show how desperate he was becoming.

She'd called him twice, but he hadn't answered. Had he gone downstairs to his office? Maddie wandered out to Jake's living area in search of him.

She spotted him beside one of the long windows, sprawled in a recliner, one hand resting on the back of the ugly three-legged cat draped across his right thigh. Head back, mouth open, Jake was snoring softly.

During her deployment, Maddie had heard plenty of snoring. It wasn't just the patients she'd heard, but the male doctors and nurses she'd worked with in a place where accommodations had often been primitive and privacy a joke. But while none of those whuffles and snorts had ever aroused even a smidgen of tender feeling in her, Jake's snoring caused a painful tightening in her chest.

Maddie crept closer. Admiring the way the dark crescents of Jake's lashes rested on his bronzed cheeks, she marveled that such a strong, confident man could look so sweetly vulnerable in sleep. Her fingers itched to smooth back the dark hair that swooped across his forehead. She wished she had the right to brush her thumb over the faint lines bracketing his mouth, perhaps provoking him to smile in his sleep.

Tripod raised his head and regarded her with impersonal curiosity, reminding her that she didn't belong here.

Jake hadn't wanted her to come. He couldn't have made that plainer. He didn't want to talk about Noah and he wasn't remotely interested in getting to know Maddie again.

With a heavy heart she returned to the kitchen and removed the second place setting from the table. She finished tidying up and then took a notepad out of her purse and wrote a message for Jake, telling him there was a tossed salad in the refrigerator, ziti with sausage and a loaf of garlic bread keeping warm in the oven, and some black-cherry ice cream in the freezer.

She put the note beside his plate and laid the change from his grocery money next to it. Then she slipped quietly down the stairs, leaving Jake alone, just as he'd wanted.

Chapter Three

So much for last night's resolution to leave him alone, Maddie thought wryly as she made a loose fist and rapped on the half-open door of Jake's office.

He lifted his gaze from the screen of his laptop computer. "Madeline. Come in." His chair squeaked as he pushed it back and stood.

She advanced a step into the office, furnished in the same elegantly threadbare style as the reception area, then glanced nervously over her shoulder. "Your secretary told me to—"

"It's fine. Come in." Jake nodded to indicate the large envelope she held like a shield in front of her. "What can I do for you?"

The envelope was a flimsy excuse for being here, Maddie realized belatedly. She should have left it with his secretary. Now there was nothing to do but plunge ahead. "I've been helping Anna review some medical files for Children of the Day. As I was leaving, she asked me to deliver this."

"Thanks." Jake accepted the envelope and dropped it unceremoniously on his desk, which held so many papers, folders, and books that Maddie couldn't see an inch of bare wood anywhere. She found something oddly endearing about the fact that after all his years in the military, where order and efficiency had been relentlessly drilled into him, Jake could work at such a messy desk.

"I planned to call you today," he said. "Can you spare a minute?" He gestured toward a leather wing chair and waited for Maddie to sit down before resuming his own seat.

He cleared his throat. "I would have called this morning, but I had to be in court early. I—" He broke off to scowl at Tripod, who had hopped onto the arm of Maddie's chair and was looking at her expectantly. "Sorry. He thinks he owns that chair. Just give him a shove."

"There's room for both of us." Maddie drew the cat onto her lap and felt oddly pleased when he settled against her.

Jake leaned forward and folded his arms on a stack of papers. "About last night, I—"

"Jake, Judge Newcastle has moved up the hearing for—" The stunning, dark-haired, blue-eyed man who had just barged into the office stopped speaking as Jake glanced pointedly in Maddie's direction.

"Oh. Sorry." The man flashed Maddie a bright smile accompanied by a killer set of dimples. "I thought he was alone."

Jake leaned back in his chair. "Madeline Bright, allow me to introduce the second-best lawyer on Veterans Boulevard. My partner, Travis Wylie."

"No, don't get up," Travis said when Maddie tried to shift Tripod so she could rise from the chair and shake hands. "Jake's ugly cat looks comfortable."

Maddie wanted to protest that Tripod wasn't ugly, but that

was an indefensible position. "He's a very nice cat," she temporized, cuddling him closer.

Travis smiled again, and Maddie marveled. With that chiseled jaw and those vibrant blue eyes, the man was even better-looking than Jake. But in his western shirt, Wranglers, and boots, he looked more like a cowboy than a lawyer.

"Madeline's an army nurse," Jake said. "Hails from Dallas."

Travis's eyes widened suddenly. He looked at Jake, raised his eyebrows as though in a question and mouthed a word that looked like "allergy."

Jake glowered at him.

Travis barked out a laugh, then turned a look of frank admiration on Maddie.

"She's come to Fort Bonnell for additional medical training," Jake said calmly, as though the conversation hadn't just taken that weird little detour. "She wants to switch from emergency nursing to maternity."

Travis perched on the arm of a chair. "How do you like Prairie Springs?" he asked, swinging one long, denim-clad leg.

Maddie's smile came easily. "It's a wonderful town. And I've found a great bunch of Christians here. Do you know Prairie Springs Christian Church? The big stone building next to the town green?"

Travis shot a glance at Jake. "Gloria, our office manager, goes there."

"Are you talking about Gloria Ridge?" Maddie asked eagerly. "She's one of my new friends. I love her sense of humor."

"Oh, she's a character," Travis agreed.

"Travis." Lexi McNally, the pencil-thin, Hollywoodblond secretary stood in the doorway. "Sorry to interrupt, but the court reporter just arrived and they're ready to start the Henley deposition."

"On my way." Travis hopped off the chair and turned another devastating smile on Maddie. "It's been a pleasure."

She murmured something equally polite and watched him go.

"Madeline." Jake unbuttoned the collar of his white dress shirt and tugged on his tie until it hung limply from a mangled knot. "About last night, I'm sorry I—"

"Please don't," she said quickly. She couldn't let him apologize for last night's date-that-wasn't-a-date. Not when she had forced her company on him. "I wasn't offended, Jake. Your leg was hurting and I'm sure you needed the rest."

His eyes softened. "I enjoyed the meal. But it wasn't right that you didn't get to eat any of it."

"Oh, I ate. I can't cook without tasting, so by the time I sit down at the table, I'm usually not hungry anymore." She grinned. "Although I did have my heart set on that black-cherry ice cream. It's my favorite." She thought she'd struck just the right note with that response; she had also left an opening for Jake to invite her to share the rest of the ice cream.

He just smiled. "It was good. Thanks for all you did."

Maddie concealed her disappointment by giving Tripod another cuddle. When she looked up, Jake was pulling documents out of Anna's envelope, his long hands moving gracefully as he sifted the papers. When he paused to read something, Maddie studied his furrowed brow and pursed lips and felt a little thrill at the realization that she was actually watching him work. She was incredibly proud of all he had accomplished. In her eyes he was even more heroic now than he'd been as a daring young helicopter pilot.

"Anna tells me you were a huge help in getting Ali to Texas," she said.

"That was simple enough," he said without looking up. "We just petitioned for a managing conservatorship and requested an emergency ex parte order. The judge granted it the same day."

Maddie stroked Tripod's back as she struggled to translate that. "So in plain English, General Willis is now Ali's legal guardian."

"No." Jake tossed the papers aside. "In Texas guardianship is handled through probate court. As Guardian of the Person, the general would have to file annual reports to prove he was acting in the boy's best interests. With a permanent managing conservatorship, we get out from under all that. Of course the general's conservatorship is just temporary right now, but we'll go back to court at the end of this month to finalize things."

"And you expect that to go well?"

"No reason it shouldn't. The judge has appointed an ad litem to discover what's in Ali's best interests and make recommendations to the court. But both parents are deceased, there are no other interested relatives, and anyone who knows the general knows he'll take good care of Ali. So we're fine."

Jake unbuttoned his cuffs and began rolling up his shirt-sleeves. "None of this is confidential, by the way. The general's grateful to everyone who had a hand in delivering his grandson into his care, so he's authorized me to answer any questions y'all might have."

"That's…very generous."

Jake looked at her. "You sound surprised."

"Not surprised, exactly." Maddie didn't like saying unkind things behind people's backs, but concern for Ali forced her to speak up. "Granted, I've just seen the man a few times, but he strikes me as a little…gruff."

She didn't believe for a minute that the retired three-star general, a bear of a man even if he *was* older than dirt, would abuse or neglect Ali. But surely the boy needed a gentler hand. "It's just that Ali's such a timid child. And he's only five."

Jake finished his sleeve-rolling and linked his hands together behind his head. "They're doing fine together. I saw them just the other day."

Maddie hadn't seen Ali in almost two weeks. She was just one of a crowd of people interested in the boy, so she worried about overwhelming him, especially as he was sick and also dealing with culture shock. "I hate to think of him being dragged into a courtroom," she said.

"Ali?" Jake shook his head. "We won't need him at the hearing."

Jake's assurances helped put her mind to rest, but Tripod comforted her also, Maddie realized as she continued to stroke his soft fur. She'd never been a cat lover, but the gentle vibrations of Tripod's purring were oddly soothing.

Jake gathered up Anna's papers and returned them to the envelope. "Just how serious is Ali's medical condition?" he asked.

"Extremely." Maddie sighed. "The bomb blast caused trauma to his heart, resulting in a ventricular septal tear. In other words, he has a hole in his heart. He's being closely monitored, and as you probably know, Dr. Nora Blake is standing by to do the surgery in Austin."

When Jake opened his mouth, Maddie anticipated his question. "She's the best, Jake. She has a tremendous reputation."

"But why is she stalling? Why hasn't she done the surgery already?"

"Because there's still a chance Ali's heart might heal on its own, and that would be best. Dr. Blake wants to wait. And Ali's not yet as strong as she'd like for the surgery, anyway."

Jake frowned, and Maddie worried that he'd press her for more information about the surgery—specifically its mortality rate. She'd looked into that last month, and now wished she hadn't.

She gave him a reassuring smile. "But even if he ends up having the surgery, there's every reason to believe things will go well."

"You always did look on the bright side of things." Jake's tone hinted at disapproval.

Maddie wondered what he'd think if he knew how the events of the past year had crushed her old optimism. "I'm sure he'll be fine," she said firmly, wishing that was the truth. "We'll just have to keep praying."

Jake's frown deepened. "I prefer to deal in reality."

So they were back to *that*. Maddie wondered just how far his doubts extended. "You don't believe in prayer?"

He stared at her for several seconds before he answered in clipped words that discouraged further comment, "Not anymore."

Maddie knew there was a world of pain behind that admission, so Jake's bitterness didn't really shock her. But he desperately needed to talk to someone, and if she could just figure out how to reestablish their old camaraderie, he might talk to *her.*

She checked her watch, then set Tripod on the floor and got to her feet. "I'm on duty at the hospital in a little over an hour, so I'd better get back to post and grab something to eat."

There. She couldn't have made it any clearer that she was available for a quick lunch. That made things nice and convenient for Jake, who was probably still feeling a bit guilty about last night.

To her dismay, he didn't even nibble at the bait. He grabbed his cane and escorted her to the door, thanking her again for bringing the papers from Anna.

Disappointment lodged in Maddie's throat, making speech difficult, so she just nodded and went on her way.

An hour after Maddie left his office, Jake was still having trouble keeping his mind on his work. He decided to make a few more notes on an immigration case, then go upstairs and clear his head with a long workout on his rowing machine. Maybe after that, he'd have some black-cherry ice cream.

Or maybe he would just throw the ice cream out.

He wished Maddie hadn't told him it was her favorite flavor. The only thing he wanted to know about Madeline Bright was that she was safe and happy. Apart from that, he didn't want to see, didn't want to hear, didn't want to *think* about her at all.

"Jake?"

He glanced up as Gloria Ridge strode into his office and pointed an accusing finger at Tripod, who had reclaimed his favorite chair after Maddie's departure. "His Highness doesn't like that fancy new food I bought." Gloria rested her hands on her wide hips and looked at Jake expectantly over the tops of her glasses.

Jake calmly turned a page and made a note on his legal pad. "If he's hungry, he'll eat it."

"Hah." Gloria's short gray curls bounced as she shook her head. "*You* were hungry yesterday, but did you eat that chili I brought in for you and Travis? No, you did not. You both turned up your noses because I put beans in it. And you like beans."

"Not in chili. No self-respecting Texan does." He couldn't believe she didn't know that. She might have been raised in Alabama, but that was no excuse. Not when she'd been married to a Texan—a retired rodeo cowboy, no less—for almost as long as Jake had been alive. Was Leland Ridge aware that his wife was going around putting beans in chili?

Gloria walked over to Tripod's chair and bent down to stroke him, muttering, "You contrary thing."

Unsure whether she was addressing him or the cat, Jake shook his head and made another note on his tablet.

Gloria turned a speculative gaze on him. "Travis says Maddie Bright came by while I was at lunch."

Here it comes. Jake did his best to rein in his exasperation. Gloria was always pushing nice women at him because she thought it was a crime against nature for a man to be almost forty and still unmarried. Jake never talked about his past, so she didn't know he was a widower.

"You're interested," Gloria guessed.

"No, ma'am," he said firmly.

Gloria laughed. "You're a lying dog." She paused, then asked silkily, "Have you kissed her yet?"

"Gloria." Appalled by the blunt question, Jake dropped

his ballpoint pen and gave his office manager a hard look. "Cease and desist."

She waved that order away with a pudgy hand. "Travis told me all about you being 'allergic' to that sweet girl."

Jake eyed the silver-handled ebony cane propped against his desk and fantasized about beating his loose-lipped partner with it.

Gloria shook her head pityingly. "You are one clueless man, Jake Hopkins."

"What I am is *busy*." The instant the words were out, he felt guilty for speaking to a woman, especially one his mama's age, so harshly. But rather than looking crushed, Gloria laughed at him, at which point Jake scrapped his plans for an apology.

"What's this?" Gloria's mirth subsided as she stepped closer to Jake's desk and bent down in front of it. When she bobbed back up, she held out a small gold woman's watch for his inspection.

"It looks familiar," Jake said. "It might be Madeline's."

Gloria pinned him with a look of intense curiosity. "Why don't you call her Maddie like everyone else does?"

"Because I've known her since she was seven years old."

Gloria snorted. "What kind of answer is that?"

The only kind of answer she was going to get. She could take it or leave it. Jake pressed his intercom button. "Lexi, somebody dropped a woman's watch in my office. Is it yours?"

His secretary answered in the negative. He thanked her and looked at Gloria. "I'll take care of it." He didn't want to call Madeline, but if he asked Gloria to do it, she'd wonder—out loud—why he was so reluctant to make a simple phone call.

Gloria laid the watch on a stack of papers on the corner

of the desk. "I've been getting to know Maddie at church. She's perfect for you."

Jake studied the watch, so diminutive compared to his own, but that made sense because Maddie's wrists were nearly as small as a child's. Which reminded him: "She's too young, Gloria."

"Hogwash. That girl has more maturity in her little finger than you and me and this cat put together. I repeat—she's perfect for you."

Jake bristled at the heavy-handed matchmaking attempt. "She's twenty-six," he said evenly. "And I'm thirty-nine."

Gloria harrumphed. "What does that matter? She's *special,* Jake. And a couple of the young men at church are interested, so I hope you get over your age fixation right quick. At least put an engagement ring on her finger so she won't wander off while you're waiting for her to get old and wrinkled enough to suit you!"

The thought of marriage to Maddie caused Jake's brain to stall out, so by the time a scathing retort rose to his lips, Gloria had already left his office.

He tamped down his impatience. Gloria wasn't the only person who wanted to see him married. His mama introduced the subject at every opportunity, usually as a prelude to some wistful comment about grandchildren. But even if Jake wanted to marry again—and he emphatically did not—the absolute last candidate he would ever consider was Madeline Bright.

If she ever discovered what he had done, she might eventually find it in her generous heart to forgive him. But how could she ever *forget?*

The kindest thing Jake could do for Maddie was stay out of her life.

* * *

Two days later, Jake wryly reflected that staying out of Maddie's life would be a whole lot easier if she'd stay on post where she belonged and not come into Prairie Springs every chance she got. He'd been ambling toward the drugstore when he stopped to get a better look at a torque wrench in the hardware store's display window. A sixth sense warned him to look over his shoulder, and he spotted the beautiful bane of his existence tripping merrily toward him.

Hurrying past the window, Jake ducked inside the hardware store. He flattened himself next to the wall so he wouldn't be in the way of anyone entering or exiting, but could still observe the sidewalk and judge when the coast was clear.

He waited for what must have been a full minute, but she didn't appear. She might not have been coming this far down the street, although knowing Maddie—*Madeline*—she had probably just stopped to brighten someone's day.

Well. Since he was here, he might as well have a look at that torque wrench. He turned away from the window and found himself facing a willowy young woman with electric-blue streaks in her black hair.

She smiled invitingly. "Welcome to Nail World."

"Nail World," Jake echoed, uncomprehending as he looked past her. What kind of hardware store had mirrored walls and bubblegum-pink carpet? When he spotted a bored-looking woman with her fingertips immersed in a bowl of sudsy water, awareness finally seeped into his Maddie-dulled brain. He'd missed the hardware store and entered the place next to it.

"Did you want a manicure right now or did you want to schedule one for another time?" the blue-haired female inquired.

A manicure. Jake almost snorted. Wouldn't Travis bust a gut laughing if he returned to the office sporting shiny pink fingernails?

"Uh, I guess I don't have time for a manicure, after all," he said, backing toward the door. "Excuse me." He turned and wrenched the door open. As he thrust himself outside, he nearly collided with Maddie.

"Jake!" She beamed a smile that made his toes wriggle inside his shoes.

"Madeline. Sorry. I wasn't looking where I was going." He made a mental note to have his prescriptions delivered to the office from now on. The streets of Prairie Springs were no longer safe.

She looked bright and pretty in a short white skirt and a yellow T-shirt that fit her like a second skin but still managed to look demure because it was edged with ruffles.

Amusement tugged at the corners of her mouth as she nodded toward the shop Jake had just escaped from. "Did you get a manicure?"

"Not hardly. I was just, uh, visiting a client who works there." He hated playing fast and loose with the truth, but what else could he say? Why did every interaction with this woman have to be so complicated?

In the bright sun her blue eyes sparkled like the clear waters of a Hill Country lake. "This kind of heat shouldn't be legal," she said cheerfully, fanning her face with a slender hand. "I just heard on the radio that it's over a hundred again, so I decided to treat myself to an ice-cream cone." She nodded toward the Creamery, the old-fashioned ice-cream parlor next to the town's green. "Want to come?"

Of course he wanted to. But he wasn't *going* to. "Sorry. I have to get right back to the office."

"Oh." Her smile faltered and her gaze skittered away.

"Another time," Jake said, hating himself for stomping all over her sunny mood.

She bit a corner of her bottom lip and nodded slowly, clearly unconvinced that the rain check he'd just handed her was bona fide. She was right to be skeptical, and Jake felt lower than a snake's belly.

"Jake…" Tilting her head to one side, she appealed to him with a look that pushed towering waves of guilt through him. "Why do you always—" She stopped and shook her head. "Never mind. You're in a hurry." She smiled again, but the sparkle had gone from her eyes. She lifted a hand and waggled her fingers. "Bye."

Her step was less sprightly as she walked away. Jake watched until she disappeared into the ice-cream parlor, then he sighed. How was he going to discourage her interest in him without crushing her spirit? And just what did she see in him, anyway? Half the time he wasn't even nice to her.

What she needed was a boyfriend. Someone young and fun, but safe. Someone who would make her feel special. Someone like…

Jake felt his mouth curve into a satisfied smile. He gave his cane a jaunty twirl and continued on his way, whistling.

Travis Wylie would do just fine.

Early on Saturday morning Maddie groped for the jangling alarm clock beside her bed and smacked the snooze button.

She'd been dreaming about Jake. He'd been sitting beside her in church, and when she'd glanced down to see the strong hand holding hers, she'd been dazzled by the flash of a diamond ring on her finger.

"Yeah, *right,*" she murmured, amused at herself for scripting such an unrealistic scene. Eyes still closed, she rolled over and hugged her pillow. She'd dearly love to be Jake's girlfriend, but she'd never given any thought to marriage. And Jake didn't even *go* to church.

The alarm went off again, jarring her out of a pleasant doze, and she got up. As had become her habit, she shuffled to the desk in her tiny, army-furnished bedroom and sat down in front of her laptop computer. Shoving a tangle of hair back from her face, she hit a key and waited for her e-mail program to come up.

"Please, Lord," she whispered. There just had to be a message from Whitney.

There was no message, but Maddie didn't have time for tears this morning. At eight o'clock she and her preceptor, a wise if somewhat stiff-necked civilian nurse named Myrna Alsop, were to meet with the hospital's head nurse and the OB supervisor to fine-tune Maddie's training program.

Maddie was convinced she'd made the right decision in switching her specialty. No longer did her workdays involve gunshot wounds and limbs blown off by rocket-propelled grenades. Now she nursed happy expectant mothers on a floor where Brahms's *Lullaby* was played over the public-address system several times a day—each time another precious baby came wriggling and squalling into the world.

It wasn't always fun; she'd had some heartbreaking cases. Just yesterday she'd helped deliver a stillborn baby and then held the sobbing young woman in her arms while Myrna placed a phone call to the soldier-husband who was serving his country on the other side of the world. But this was everyday life, not war, and the work was deeply satisfying.

Just as Whitney had told her it would be.

The meeting was productive but brief, and things were slow on the ward, so Maddie worried about Whitney all morning. On her lunch break she thought about phoning Whitney's brother, a local rancher, and she thought about calling army chaplain Steve Windham, a good man who had been involved in bringing Ali Willis to Texas. But when she picked up the phone in the nurses' lounge, it was Anna Terenkov's number that she entered. Children of the Day had contacts in the region where Whitney and John had disappeared, so Maddie suspected Anna might be the first person in Prairie Springs to hear anything.

"I'm sorry to bother you again," Maddie began when Anna answered. "I know you said you'd call me if you heard anything, but I just—"

"We still don't have any news." Anna's tone was saturated with regret. "Nothing at all, Maddie. I'm sorry."

Maddie closed her eyes and nodded. At least Anna didn't have any *bad* news, and that meant they could keep hoping and praying.

Maddie wasn't sure there was much hope left in her, but she could still pray. Alone in the nurses' lounge, she hung up the phone and bowed her head.

After spending a frustrating and wholly unproductive Monday morning at the county courthouse in Austin, Jake tossed his suit coat and briefcase onto the passenger seat of his BMW. He stowed his cane, then settled into the driver's seat and peeled out of the parking lot, top down and country music CD blaring.

Jake's father had always maintained that George Strait had a song to fit just about any situation in a man's life. George was real Texas, honest as the day was long, and had a mellow voice that just wouldn't quit. By the time Jake had listened to half a dozen of George's toe-tappers and swerved to avoid nearly as many dead armadillos on the blazing-hot highway, he was back in Prairie Springs and in a better mood.

He had just set to work sorting the phone messages that had stacked up during his absence when he heard a familiar two-beat knock on his half-open office door. Guessing what his partner wanted, he spoke without looking up. "No. I can't get away."

"You're not so important that you can't take thirty minutes for lunch." Travis nudged the door open with his elbow and strolled into the office, buttoning a blue-and-white-checked dress shirt that Jake had washed and ironed just last night.

"New shirt?" Jake asked dryly.

Travis grinned, showing the dimples that drove women wild. "Spilled coffee on mine. Good thing your closet's right upstairs. But I couldn't find any western shirts."

Jake raised an eyebrow at him. "This is probably a new concept to somebody who grew up rich, Wylie, but beggars can't be choosers."

Travis shrugged and tucked the shirt into his jeans. Like Jake, he wore suits only in court. That sorely disappointed the female population of Prairie Springs, because while Travis in jeans, boots and a Resistol hat made women sigh, Travis in one of his designer suits made them swoon.

Jake made a mental note to arrange for Maddie to see Travis in a suit. She'd sure forget *him* fast enough.

"Let's go to Charlie's," Travis said.

It was tempting. The beef brisket Charlie lovingly smoked and slow-cooked over a hickory-wood fire was the best in all of Texas. But if Jake didn't get started on his calls, he wouldn't have a hope of getting back to everyone within the twenty-four hours he always promised. Resolutely shaking his head, he picked up his phone.

"Would it influence your decision if I told you I just saw Gloria in the kitchen heatin' up a pan of that awful chili she brought in the other day?" Travis asked.

"Absolutely." Jake put down the phone and reached for his cane.

Travis pushed his fingers through the dark waves of his hair. Jake winced inwardly as he imagined Maddie's fingers doing that while she kissed Travis. But the fact that he was disturbed by that image only emphasized the urgency of getting her and Travis together. If the woman persisted in walking around unattached, Jake might slip up and kiss her himself.

"Jake and I will be at Charlie's," Travis called to Lexi as he plucked his cowboy hat off the coat tree in the hall. He settled the hat on his head and opened the front door, then turned to wait for Jake. "Think you could hurry up, there, Hopalong? I'm starving."

"I'm coming," Jake grumbled, limping a little faster. He didn't bother objecting to the nickname, which the irreverent Travis had bestowed on him back in their law-school days at the University of Texas. He supposed Hopkins did sound a little like Hopalong, as in Hopalong Cassidy, the old-time movie cowboy who limped.

On the three-block jaunt to the edge of downtown, Jake and Travis discussed an adoption case Jake was working on for Children of the Day. But as Travis pulled open the dilapidated screen door of Charlie's Bar-B-Q, Jake introduced a new subject.

"Trav, what was your impression of Madeline Bright?"

Travis stopped in the doorway to look at him. "That she'd be an allergy worth havin'."

That reminded Jake. "Thanks for sharing that with Gloria," he said sourly. "If this wasn't one of my favorite canes, I'd break it over your sorry head."

"Hey," Travis said with an air of aggrieved innocence. "She was jawin' at me about marriage. A man has to protect himself."

"By sacrificing his friends?"

Travis shrugged. "I'm a little hard-pressed to feel sorry for you, Hopalong. If Madeline Bright was makin' eyes at *me*, I sure wouldn't be avoidin' her. That woman's as pretty as a field of bluebonnets."

"Glad you think so," Jake said as they stepped inside. "Because I want you to ask her out."

Travis halted mid-mosey and eyed him with suspicion. "Why's that?"

Jake shrugged. "She's new in town." He made his way to the serving counter, uncomfortably aware that he had just suggested Maddie was friendless when, in fact, she never met a stranger. By all accounts, she'd charmed half the population of Prairie Springs within hours of her arrival.

"Hey, Charlie," Jake greeted the grizzly old man behind the serving counter.

Looking up from the rack of beef ribs he was splitting, Charlie waved his huge carving knife. "Hey, boys." His wide mouth opened in a grin that displayed a row of tobacco-stained teeth. "How's the law business?"

"Could be better," Travis said cheerfully as Jake grabbed two trays and slapped them on the counter. "So we're fixin' to change the brass plaque by our front door."

Jake turned to stare at him.

"Yep." Travis stuffed his hands into the pockets of his jeans and rocked back on his heels. "We're thinkin' we might attract more clients if our plaque said, 'Hopkins and Wylie, Good ol' Boys at Law.'"

Charlie's guffaw was so loud it turned every head in the place. Still grinning, he applied himself to cutting slices from the huge slab of mahogany-colored beef that sat on a scarred cutting board.

Travis leaned toward Jake to continue their private discussion. "Why don't *you* take her out? She looks harmless enough."

"I'm not afraid of her," Jake retorted. "I'm just too old for her." At thirty-four, Travis was no kid, either. But he acted like one, and that put him a lot closer to Maddie's age.

Travis gave him a long, speculative look. "Now that's real interesting, the way you put that. I wonder why you didn't say she's too young for you?"

Jake frowned. "It's the same thing."

"Nuh-uh." Travis shook his head emphatically. "For some reason, you're lookin' at things from her perspective, instead of your own. And as I said, that's real interesting."

Jake didn't bother to hide his exasperation. "What did you do, Wylie, find a psychology degree in your cereal box this morning?"

Behind the counter, Charlie handed a sturdy disposable

plate piled with beef to his plump little wife, Virginia. She looked inquiringly at Travis and waited for him to choose his side dishes.

"I'll have pinto beans and potato salad, thank you, ma'am." Travis sent her a broad wink. "Have you done something different to your hair? Looks good."

"Oh, hush up," the old lady said as her wrinkled face flushed with pleasure. Struggling to hide a smile, she pushed a serving spoon into a tub of potato salad.

Jake leaned toward Travis and spoke for his ears alone. "I've known Madeline since she was in the first grade. I'm just looking out for her, that's all." He waited while Travis thanked Virginia and flattered her some more, then added, "Just ask her out, Trav. You won't be sorry."

Travis turned to look at him. "No, but *you* might be."

"Not as long as you treat her like a lady." Jake hesitated, then couldn't stop himself from adding, "I'll need your word on that."

"Real interesting," Travis said again. With his thumb he nudged his hat back on his head. "I guess you'll be wantin' me to go ahead and marry her, too."

"What I *want* is for you to be serious for once," Jake snapped. "Think you can manage that?"

Travis slapped a hand against his chest and widened his eyes. "Partner, I'm as serious as a heart attack."

Jake snorted in disgust, then noticed Virginia was waiting for him to order his sides. He gave her an apologetic smile and chose potato salad, coleslaw and some throat-searing sweet-hot pickles.

Travis paid for their meals and they sat down at a picnic table under one of the slow-moving paddle fans suspended from the high ceiling. The sticky-topped table held a roll of cheap paper towels, two long plastic sleeves of crackers and a squirt-top bottle of barbecue sauce. A red smear of sauce on the table was being buzzed by a couple of flies, but Jake was satisfied with the ambience of the place. He didn't mind the lack of air-conditioning or the peeling paint on the old brick walls. As his father had always said, frills in a barbecue joint gave a man reason to suspect the proprietors weren't lavishing enough attention on their meat.

"I don't see why it's so all-fired important for me to take her out," Travis said as he emptied sugar packets into his iced tea. "Not that I'd mind, you understand. But a pretty little thing like that isn't likely to have any trouble attractin' men."

"She doesn't have any trouble attracting men," Jake admitted. He just needed to get her interested in somebody other than himself, and Travis was the safest distraction. Sometimes Travis could be as annoying as a toothache, but he wouldn't break Maddie's heart. "I'm just trying to make sure she doesn't wind up with a jerk."

Travis choked on a mouthful of tea and put his cup down with a thump. "Jake? Did you just compliment me?"

"Not on purpose," Jake muttered. He took a long pull from his bottle of root beer and returned to business. "I know y'all just met the one time, but I've mentioned your name and I might have accidentally flattered you, so I think she'll accept your invitation. Take her somewhere nice, like maybe to that new seafood—"

Travis silenced him with a raised hand. "Thanks for the advice, Hopalong, but this ain't exactly my first rodeo."

Jake ignored the sarcasm. "Just treat her right or you'll answer to me."

Travis reached for the plastic squirt bottle and applied barbecue sauce to his beef. "Mighty protective, aren't you?"

Jake had hoped to avoid this, but it was becoming clear that he'd have to reveal some of the truth in order to secure Travis's cooperation. "Her brother was my best friend," Jake said quietly, hoping that was explanation enough.

It appeared to be. Travis's jaw dropped and every trace of levity vanished from his expression.

Jake considered the man across the table a good friend, but he'd told Travis next to nothing about his life before law school, where they'd met. He was aware that Travis had gleaned a few details, mostly from times when Jake's mother had said too much in front of him. But Jake didn't discuss his past, ever. His old life was dead, just like Noah.

Travis continued to regard him with unabashed fascination. "You're talking about the guy who was killed when your helicopter went down."

Jake nodded. "Noah Bright." After all this time, saying the name out loud was as hard as swallowing sand.

"So you're lookin' after Noah's sister." Travis appeared to mull that over as he addressed his beef with a plastic knife and fork. "And that's your only interest in her."

Jake didn't care for the insinuation in his tone. "What other interest could I have? There's thirteen years between us." Not to mention that load of guilt Jake had been hauling around since Noah's death.

Instead of answering, Travis poked a forkful of meat into his mouth. He chewed with annoying equanimity, watching Jake all the while.

Jake waited, tension curling his right hand into a fist. If Travis said "real interesting" just one more time, it was going to require every atom of Jake's self-control not to flatten him.

Travis raised one mocking eyebrow. "I guess you'd better give me her number, then."

"When we get back to the office," Jake promised. Not that he needed to look it up. He had never phoned Maddie, but a few weeks ago she'd given him her number, and it just happened to stick in his mind.

That was the whole problem, Jake reflected as he picked up his fork and pushed at his food, his appetite gone. Everything about Madeline Bright stuck in his mind.

She was going to be a hard woman to forget.

Chapter Four

She was stalking him.

No, Jake swiftly corrected himself, she wouldn't do that. The woman was as sweet and as guileless as a pink-frosted cupcake. There was a reasonable explanation for the fact that he saw her everywhere he went. This was a small town, and he and Maddie—*Madeline*—knew a lot of the same people. One of those people was little Ali Willis, so Jake shouldn't have been surprised to see the bright-yellow Ford Escape parked in General Willis's circular driveway.

He glanced at his watch and sighed, wishing he could just hit the gas and shoot past the Georgian-style brick mansion. But he was already three minutes late for a meeting with the general, who was a stickler for punctuality, so he parked behind Maddie's SUV. With any luck, she'd never know he'd stopped by. The house was enormous, and Jake was here to see the old man, not Ali.

General Marlon Willis had long since retired, but he still possessed a proud military bearing and a keen gaze capable of striking terror into the heart of any man he outranked, which was pretty much everybody except a handful of other generals and the president of the United States. The old man had taken a shine to Jake, so in addition to handling the matter of the managing conservatorship, Jake was updating the general's will and looking into a couple of his investments.

Jake buttoned his suit coat, then grabbed his silver-handled ebony stick and his briefcase and headed to the mansion's front door. His ring was answered almost immediately by the gray-haired housekeeper. She recognized Jake and informed him the general was waiting in his study.

Jake thanked her and made his way to the end of the high-ceilinged hall, where he knocked on a six-panel door.

"Enter," the general barked.

The old man was seated behind his desk and talking on the phone. As usual he was in full western dress, his hat hanging on a rack of deer antlers mounted on the wall behind him. Nodding politely, Jake crossed the room to stand before one of the windows overlooking a lush garden that was quite an achievement, given the hot, dry summers of central Texas.

Through the glass he heard the peaceful splashing of a fountain. He also caught the muffled sound of childish giggles interspersed with the dulcet tones of the woman he hadn't yet succeeded in banishing from his dreams.

Several large soap bubbles floated past the window. When more little-boy giggles were followed by Maddie's rich laughter, Jake fought and conquered his answering smile.

"Sorry to keep you waiting," General Willis said.

Jake turned. "That's quite all right, sir." He laid his briefcase on a leather sofa and unlatched it. As he removed a file folder, he nodded toward the window. "Sounds like Ali's in good spirits today."

"We both are. Having my grandson here is doing wonders for my heart."

"I'm delighted to hear that, sir." Jake wondered whether the man's reference to his heart had been figurative or literal. The last time they'd met, the general had seemed short of breath. Today his complexion could be characterized as florid. Did that indicate some kind of heart problem? Jake didn't know, and it certainly wasn't his place to ask.

The boy, of course, was a different matter. Jake again glanced toward the window. "Speaking of hearts, has Ali's surgery been scheduled yet?"

"It's set for next week." Worry clouded the old man's eyes. "Dr. Blake has waited as long as she dares. We were hoping the injury would begin to heal on its own, but the most recent electrocardiogram showed that isn't happening." The general's gnarled hand trembled slightly as he pushed it through his thick white hair.

"I'm sure the surgery will go well," Jake said politely, although he wasn't sure at all. It wasn't like him to encourage false hopes, but he'd been seeing too much of Maddie lately, and her relentless optimism had begun to erode his pragmatic approach to life. "Madeline Bright says Dr. Blake is the best," he offered.

"Madeline Bright." The general's expression lightened as he repeated the name. "Now there's a sweet little girl."

"Yes, sir." Jake could hardly have answered that comment any other way, but the old man's shrewd gaze sharpened on him.

"Any interest in that direction?"

"No, sir." Jake gave strength to his denial by shaking his head and adding, "Not my type."

A smile played on the general's mouth. "Well, you'd best be careful, Hopkins. A girl like that could change a man's type for good."

"Yes, sir," Jake said tonelessly. He opened his folder and extracted some papers.

"To business, then." The general held out his hand for the papers.

As Jake approached the desk, Maddie's low laugh rippled just outside the window. General Willis smiled when he heard it, but Jake kept his expression carefully blank.

Ali was a quiet boy, both by nature and because his heart condition had robbed him of the boundless energy most five-year-olds possessed. As Maddie sat facing him on the spongy grass of the general's backyard, his shy smile warmed her heart. He'd been in low spirits when she arrived, but she had made him laugh.

That was her special talent, cheering people up. She'd been practicing it for most of her life, thanks to Noah. As she watched Ali dip the little wand into the bottle of soap bubbles she'd brought him, she remembered a hot day just like this when *she* was five years old. She'd blown soap bubbles at Noah and laughed because he'd looked so funny slumped in a lawn chair with his long legs stuck in her pink plastic wading pool. He'd been holding a book on his bare chest and studying for a calculus final. But he'd looked up and smiled indulgently every time Maddie squealed that she'd blown the biggest bubble this time, the absolute biggest bubble ever.

Maddie was pulled back to the present as Ali's careful blowing produced a large bubble. When it broke free of the wand, he beamed at Maddie and said in his halting, charmingly accented English, "My bub-ble is more big than all your many bub-bles."

Maddie chuckled, and then as a light breeze caught the bubble and carried it away, her mind wandered again.

Their father had died when Maddie was a baby, so Noah, thirteen years her senior, had been the man Maddie looked up to. She'd loved him dearly and tried to make him proud.

"Are you being good, Maddie-bird?" he always wanted to know when he phoned home from West Point. "Are you keeping Mama cheered up while I'm gone?"

Noah wanted her to keep their mama cheered up, so Maddie had determined to be the best-behaved, happiest little girl in Texas. She even expanded her efforts to include cheering up friends and relatives. When she had troubles, she kept them to herself because she was Maddie-bird, the merry little girl who made sure everyone was happy.

"Three bub-bles!" Ali announced proudly when he produced three bubbles with one breath.

"That's very good." Maddie felt guilty for not giving the boy her full attention, but lately she just couldn't seem to stop thinking about Noah.

And Jake.

She plucked a stiff blade of grass and absently rolled it between her finger and thumb. Naturally she'd been devastated by Noah's death. But even as she'd grieved for him, she had honored his memory by comforting their loved ones, making them smile and even laugh as she reminded them of the happy times they'd shared with Noah.

She would have comforted Jake, too, but during his long stay in the hospital and then at the rehab center, he'd steadfastly refused all visitors except his parents.

Maddie stared down at the blade of grass and ripped it into two pieces, then four. Was Jake ever going to talk to her about Noah?

"I'm sorry to spoil the fun out here." Tilda, Ali's private nurse, bustled toward them in a starched white uniform. "But it's time for your afternoon rest, Ali."

"Your eyes *are* looking a little droopy." Maddie caressed his fine dark hair. "Will you put the lid back on the bottle, please?"

Ali did that, and then he begged and was granted permission to accompany Maddie to the front door. In the hall they encountered Jake, impeccably attired in a dark-gray suit and carrying a black leather briefcase and a shiny black cane.

"Well, if it isn't Mr. Hopkins," Maddie said playfully. "He's looking very dapper today, don't you think, Ali?"

Dark brows drew together over the boy's large brown eyes. "What is dap-per?"

Maddie grinned at Jake. "It means handsome."

"Yes, he is dap-per," Ali decided, gazing up at Jake with obvious admiration. "Howdy, Mr. Hop-kins."

Jake nodded courteously. "Howdy, Mr. Willis."

Ali tugged on Maddie's hand. When she bent toward him, he lowered his voice to a confidential tone. "This is how we greet friends in Texas."

"Ah."

"But Mr. Hop-kins is not a Texas man," Ali continued.

"He isn't?"

"I'm not?" Jake looked understandably confused by that pronouncement.

"No." Ali gave his head an emphatic shake.

"I'm as Texas as they come," Jake protested. "I have an

entire drawer filled with Longhorn T-shirts. And I have *all* of George Strait's albums."

Maddie stifled a snort of laughter. Jake's fanaticism for the University of Texas's football team and a popular country-music artist were unlikely to impress a preschooler from the Middle East.

"But you have no boots," Ali said, staring pointedly at Jake's shiny black shoes. "No hat." He shrugged an apology before adding the clincher, "You have no pickup truck."

Jake opened his mouth to respond, but just then Tilda intervened to remind Ali it was time for his nap.

Maddie kissed his pale little cheek, then walked outside with Jake.

"What has the general been teaching that kid?" Jake grumbled as the front door closed behind them. "Just because a man has never gone in for cowboy hats and tooled leather belts with silver buckles the size of turkey platters doesn't mean he's not a Texan through and through. As for my ride, my first choice would have been a pickup truck, but the Beemer's easier to get in and out of."

He was so adorably disgruntled, Maddie wanted to hug him. As they walked together, she slid a glance in his direction and was struck by the way his dark suit and the vivid blue silk of his tie set off the silver strands in his hair. She was stabbed by a sudden longing to get closer to him, so when they reached her SUV and he would have said goodbye and continued on to his own car, she impulsively touched his arm.

He stopped and turned swiftly, almost as though she'd roped him and tugged him toward her. But she didn't spend more than an instant marveling at that; she had an opportunity to seize.

"I like this pattern," she said, moving half a step closer and reaching up to straighten his tie. When she raised her eyes to his face, their gazes collided, then clung.

Maddie held her breath and waited, but nothing happened. Nervously she brushed back a lock of hair and tucked it behind her ear.

As he watched the move, Jake's mouth fell open and he drew an audible breath.

Was he going to kiss her or not? she wondered almost irritably. She thought about rising on her toes and helping to get things started, but just then Jake's mouth snapped shut and he looked down at the hand that still grasped one edge of his tie.

Wincing inwardly, Maddie withdrew her hand and stepped back. Then because she felt so awkward, she began stuffing words into the silence.

"Are you free on Saturday, by any chance? A bunch of us from church are going tubing on the Guadalupe River. It's not a couples' thing, just a group of friends. Come with us, Jake. It'll be fun." She'd managed all of that on a single breath and could only imagine how foolish she must appear to him at this moment. She couldn't quite meet his eyes, but she was aware that they'd turned as dark and unfathomable as the spaces between the stars in the night sky.

So she simply waited, bracing herself for the rejection that would surely follow her rash invitation.

Where he'd found the strength to keep from kissing her just then, Jake didn't know, but he felt faint with relief. Maddie's flushed cheeks and fast talking said clearly that he'd embarrassed her, but he could hardly apologize for that when he didn't want to get anywhere near explaining why he hadn't kissed her—or why he had *wanted* to.

So he was grateful for her chatter, and he was seriously tempted by her invitation to go tubing. He hadn't done that since high school, but the idea of lying across the inflated inner tube of a truck tire, dangling his arms and legs in the cold Guadalupe River as he was carried downstream on its slow current, held plenty of appeal. As a kid he'd whiled away more than a few summer afternoons on that river. It had been pure pleasure, floating between banks lined with cypress trees that stretched their limbs over the water to provide dappled shade from the blazing Texas sun.

He came perilously close to saying yes. But just in time, he remembered that going tubing with Maddie was out of the question for several reasons, one of them being that she would undoubtedly wear a swimsuit for the occasion.

If the mere thought of that disturbed him, how much worse would the reality be?

"I have to work," he said.

"Too bad." Her cheeks blazed pink as she turned to open her car door.

She didn't understand, but Jake could hardly explain. He longed to drop his briefcase and cane and wrap his arms around her and bury his face in her thick, glossy hair and beg the forgiveness he knew he could never deserve. But he wouldn't do that to her.

"Travis might be free," he ventured, hoping to nudge her interest in that direction. "Maybe I shouldn't repeat this, but he said you were as pretty as a field of bluebonnets."

"I'm not desperate for a date," Maddie said crisply. "I just thought it might do you some good to—"

"Okay," he said, startled by her irritation. "I'm sorry."

Standing beside her open car door, she hugged herself and looked so forlorn that Jake almost changed his mind and accepted her invitation. "I'm the one who should apologize," she said, staring at the knot of his tie. "It's just that I'm confused and frustrated, Jake. You used to *talk* to me, but now you don't."

Her moist, innocent eyes begged for something he could never give her. As guilt tightened around his heart, threatening to crush it, he looked up at the hot blue sky. "The past is *past,* Madeline."

"I think we should talk about it," she persisted.

How typically female. Why were women so big on talking? If you could solve anything by talking, then sure, Jake was all in favor of the exercise. But sometimes talking was pointless, and in *this* case, talking could hurt her irrevocably.

The very last thing Madeline Bright needed to know was the truth about how her brother had died.

"Noah's gone," Jake said firmly. "Talking about how much we miss him isn't going to make that hurt any less."

"I just think we should—"

"If you want to talk, Madeline, go find somebody who wants to talk back. I don't. I'm sorry." Feeling every inch like the unmitigated heel he was, Jake left her standing there, tears shimmering in her pretty blue eyes as he walked away as fast as he could.

Behind him, he heard the slam of her car door. She started her engine and was gone by the time he'd hurled his sorry hide into the Beemer.

He couldn't believe he'd spoken so harshly to her. But maybe she'd stop pressing him now.

As he slid his key into the ignition, he heard the low-pitched thrumming of helicopter rotors approaching from the west. He groaned, then sat back in his seat to wait. At a cruising speed of 180 miles an hour, the Apache wouldn't be overhead for long.

As the combined sounds of roaring engines and whipping rotors grew louder, Jake's traitorous bones vibrated in perfect resonance. But he didn't look up. He *would not* look up. As the low-flying gunship passed over him, he gripped the steering wheel and shut his eyes, fighting to hold on to his sanity. But his mind slipped its leash and incited every cell in his body to rebel against his will and remember.

As command pilot, he sat behind and above his copilot/gunner, so the sight of Noah's helmet bobbing in front of him was something he mostly took for granted. But when Noah's head suddenly jerked to the left, Jake's gaze followed.

"Break right!" Noah yelled.

Jake had already seen the red streak of tracer fire from an AK-47 and was all for avoiding it. But when he shoved the cyclic stick forward and to the right, dipping his ship's nose and banking sharply in that direction while pouring on some speed, they ran into more trouble. Jake's heart dropped into his belly as tracer rounds stitched through the dark sky from every direction, their broken lines of colored light pointing like accusing fingers at the Apache, making it an easy target for the other insurgents on the ground.

They'd flown straight into an ambush. In addition to the tracer bullets, they were now being hammered by antiaircraft rounds and exploding rocket-propelled grenades—as was their wingman, who radioed that he'd lost his flight-management computer and was out of control. Seconds later

Jake and Noah watched in stunned disbelief as their comrades' ship was blown apart.

It was the gentle drone of a nearby bee that called Jake back to the present. He opened his eyes, then drew a shaky breath and slowly released it.

This one had been bad.

Four years ago his flashbacks and nightmares had prompted him to do some reading on post-traumatic stress disorder. His questions answered, he had opted not to seek professional help because his condition wasn't affecting anyone but himself. He could hardly complain about the occasional flashback or nightmare; after what he had done, he deserved them.

But the symptoms he'd once thought manageable had been visiting him with alarming frequency and devastating power in the month since Maddie had arrived in Prairie Springs. Seeing her and thinking about her reminded him of his guilt, which in turn triggered the release of his carefully contained memories of the worst night of his life.

As he started the Beemer's engine, Jake renewed his resolve to avoid Madeline Bright. He was beginning to believe she was every bit as dangerous to him as he was to her.

Chapter Five

Maddie was still trying to rationalize Jake's behavior as she drove across the Prairie Springs River Bridge, which led to the main gate of Fort Bonnell. Because she knew he'd never intentionally inflict pain on anyone, especially her, she hesitated to blame him for the cruel things he'd said. But while he hadn't meant to hurt her, that was exactly what he'd done.

And the dear blockhead was oblivious to that fact.

If she stepped in front of a bus, Jake wouldn't stop to think before risking his own life to save hers. But would he talk to her about his feelings? No way. *That* was too scary. Talking about his feelings would require admitting that he had actual human emotions.

Was that such a terrifying prospect?

Shaking her head in mild disgust, she tried to put him out of her mind as she pulled up to the guard's booth and lowered her window. She showed her military ID, then drove to the nearest dining facility—known in the acronym-loving army as a DFAC—to grab some dinner.

She enjoyed cooking, but her apartment's kitchenette

wasn't suitable for anything more ambitious than making a cup of tea or popping some corn in the microwave. She'd barely had room on her tiny countertop to cut up the pineapple she'd bought for snacking. She could hardly wait to find a house and have a real kitchen where she could cook every day. Until then, she had her meal card and the DFACs.

At the serving counter, she selected a Caesar salad and tomato soup. Spotting an ER nurse she knew only by sight but who looked down in the dumps, she carried her tray over to his table and made a new friend. He was pining for his girlfriend back in Montana, Maddie learned, and was worried that she wouldn't wait for him. Maddie suggested that he stop relying solely on the telephone for communication and try sending a few handwritten love letters. He brightened considerably and said he'd try that.

Feeling a bit brighter herself, Maddie went home to finish some assigned reading for her nursing class.

An hour later, still seated at her desk in the tiny, nondescript bedroom she'd tried to cozy up with a handmade quilt and an African violet, she phoned her mother. She was free on Sunday and was thinking about driving up to Dallas after church.

"Yes, I'll be home," Marva Bright said in answer to Maddie's question. "I'm fixin' to go to the grocery store now. Why don't I pick up some black-cherry ice cream?"

"That sounds good." Twirling a lock of hair around her finger, Maddie wondered if Jake had yet eaten her share of the black-cherry ice cream in his freezer.

"Why don't you see if Jake wants to come?" her mother said. I'd love to see him, and you'd enjoy the ride in his convertible."

Maddie almost snorted. She couldn't see Jake agreeing

to embark on a two-hour drive with her in his passenger seat. He'd be too worried that she might try to persuade him to talk about his feelings. She rolled her eyes, disgusted with him all over again. "No, I don't think he…" She stopped as she realized her mother had just said something very odd. "Mama, how did you know Jake has a convertible?"

"Doesn't he?"

"Yes, but how did you know that?" Afraid her mother would read too much into her renewed interest in Jake, Maddie had said very little about him.

"You must have mentioned it, Maddie."

She screwed up her face and thought about that. "No. I'm sure I didn't."

"Well, I'm not psychic." Her mother gave an airy little chuckle. "So you *must* have."

Maddie's attention was diverted by her phone's signal that another call was waiting. "Mama, I have to go. I'll see you on Sunday."

"Are you going to invite Jake?"

"No. I'm sure he'll be busy." Busy burying all those emotions he didn't want to admit having. "Love you, Mama. 'Bye."

Maddie clicked off and answered the other call. To her surprise, she was greeted by Jake's law partner. They'd met only briefly, but recalling Travis Wylie's easy manner and quick smile, Maddie risked teasing him. "What can I do for the second-best lawyer on Veterans Boulevard?"

"Hmm." Amusement colored his tone. "I can see you're going to be a hard woman to impress, Madeline."

She smiled. "My friends call me Maddie."

"Jake doesn't."

That was something she'd been wondering about. In the old days he'd called her Maddie just like everyone else, but now he seemed to be trying to distance himself from her. "Jake's a law unto himself," she grumbled, and then wanted to slap her mouth because she'd sounded so bitter.

Travis chuckled. "He sure is. I'm scratchin' my head over the fact that while he's clearly interested in you, he told me to ask you out."

"He *told* you?" Outraged, Maddie came out of her chair. So Jake thought she needed help getting a date, did he?

"For the record, Maddie, I'd *enjoy* takin' you out. But I don't want to do that to Jake, so maybe you could just mention that I called and you weren't interested." He paused. "Unless you want to go out with me just to stir him up? 'Cause I can guarantee you, darlin', that would do the trick."

While Travis had spoken, Maddie had moved to her bedroom window and nudged the plain beige curtain aside. Now she stared at the fading orange-red streaks left behind by the setting sun and slowly shook her head.

If Travis thought she could get Jake's attention by going out with another man, then Travis had totally misread the situation. It was becoming abundantly clear that she would never be anything more to Jake than Noah's pesky little sister. No wonder he was trying to fix her up with Travis. What better way to get her off his hands?

She sighed and let the curtain fall back into place. "Thanks for the offer, Travis, but I don't play those games."

"But you're interested, aren't you? In Jake?"

She wanted to deny it, but Travis's honesty pulled the truth out of her. "Very interested." In spite of everything. "But it's a one-way street, Travis."

"I don't think so, darlin'. I don't know exactly what's goin' through that boy's mind, but he gets mighty riled up whenever your name is mentioned."

"He feels responsible for me." Trapping the phone against her ear with her shoulder, Maddie hugged herself. "It's a long story."

"I know about your brother," Travis said. "But I don't think this has anything to do with takin' care of Noah's little sister. Whatever Jake's been thinkin' about you, Maddie, it's not brotherly, if you get my drift."

"I get your drift, Travis, but you're mistaken." Restless, she wandered out to her matchbox-size, all-beige living room. Getting out of this boring little apartment and into a house of her own would do wonders for her flagging spirits.

"I don't know," Travis said after a brief silence that Maddie hadn't found at all uncomfortable. "Maybe we ought to try shaking some sense into him."

She didn't like the sound of that. "Travis, I won't go out with you just to make him jealous."

"Fine. Then go out with me because I'm rich, good-lookin' and fun to be with."

If any other man had uttered those words, Maddie would have thought him insufferably conceited. But Travis's light-hearted tone had held a note of self-mockery that made her smile. She suspected he'd be very good company. "I'm thinking about it," she admitted as she lowered herself onto her hard brown sofa.

She had no interest in provoking Jake to jealousy. She couldn't have accomplished that, in any case. But maybe having some innocent fun with a nice guy like Travis was just what she needed right now.

She pulled her legs up and tucked them under her, settling more comfortably on the sofa. And then she asked her new friend if he had ever been tubing on the Guadalupe River.

On Tuesday afternoon Maddie toured two houses. One proved too much of a fixer-upper for her limited skills and the other was beyond her financial means. Still, she'd had fun looking, and she was in an upbeat mood until she walked out to her SUV and happened to glance at her watch.

The watch was a cheap one, purchased last week because she needed a timepiece for her work. She'd bought it the day after losing the expensive gold watch that had been Noah's last gift to her. Ordered months before her twenty-first birthday, the present had been delivered to their mother for safekeeping just two weeks before Noah's death.

Maddie chided herself for mourning the loss of a mere possession when Whitney and John were missing, Ali's little heart could give out at any moment, and Jake was fighting so hard to deny his emotions and even his belief in God. But every glance at the poor substitute on her wrist thrust a shaft of pain through her heart.

She'd discovered the watch missing in the middle of her shift last Tuesday, and she'd been looking for it everywhere. She hadn't asked Jake about it, even though she'd been at his office that day, because he would have told her if he'd found it. He'd have known whose watch it was the moment he read the engraved words on the back: *Maddie-bird, you are loved. Noah.*

But what if he'd never seen the watch? What if it had fallen between the cushions of Tripod's favorite chair? Maddie wanted to kick herself for not considering that possibility before now.

She was just a few blocks from Jake's office, so with fresh hope in her heart, she drove over there and asked Lexi if anyone had found a gold watch.

"Jake found one last week," the secretary said. As the phone on her desk began to ring, she flipped her blond hair away from her face and added, "Why don't you go on back? I need to catch this call."

Maddie smiled her thanks and hurried off, too excited about getting her watch back to worry about intruding on Jake. But when she reached his office, she found the door closed.

She could hear the deep rumble of his voice through the door, but she couldn't tell whether he was talking to someone in person or on the phone. She guessed it must be the latter, since Lexi hadn't indicated he was with a client.

"Come in," Jake called in response to Maddie's timid knock.

She opened the door just enough to poke her head in. "Jake, I'm sorry to bother you, but Lexi says you found my watch."

"Oh!" His handsome face flushed. "Yes. Come in. I have it right here."

"Thank you," Maddie whispered, addressing the Lord rather than Jake, although she supposed Jake deserved some gratitude, also.

He'd risen when she'd opened the door; now he bent over his cluttered desk, looking flustered as he shifted piles of papers in an apparent search for the watch.

"Gloria found it," he said. "I was planning to call you, but I got busy and forgot. I'm sorry." He straightened, and for a moment simply allowed his gaze to wander over the mass of books and file folders as though he expected to locate the watch using X-ray vision. Suddenly he sprang forward and lifted a stack of papers from the top-right corner of the desk.

And there it was, the gleaming gold symbol of a brother's love. Jake tossed the papers aside and reached for it.

Maddie's eager hand closed around her treasure an instant before Jake got there, so his hand landed on top of hers with a soft smack. She expected him to behave as though he'd just touched a hot stove, but he didn't move, and the warmth of his palm against the back of her hand sent a little thrill shivering through Maddie. Slowly raising her eyes to his face, she found him looking almost comically perplexed.

His gaze shifted to her mouth. When his Adam's apple moved convulsively, Maddie realized with a shock that Travis had been right: not all of Jake's feelings for her were brotherly. She was unable to prevent a small, triumphant smile from curving her lips.

Jake blinked, and when he slid his hand off Maddie's, his deep, dark-brown eyes were as enigmatic as ever. "I'm sorry. It was inexcusable of me to forget I had your watch."

"You're forgiven." She expelled a small happy sigh. "I'm just so relieved that you found it. It was my last gift from—" Just in time, she stopped herself from mentioning Noah's name. The last thing she wanted right now was to provoke Jake into repeating the harsh words he'd spoken at the general's house.

Flustered, she busied herself inspecting her most prized possession. One of the small pins that joined the watch and band had slipped out, but that would be a quick, inexpensive repair.

"*Yoo-hoo!* Jake? Did you forget somebody?" A woman's muffled but plainly amused voice came from beneath a pile of papers on the desk.

Jake shifted a few things, uncovering his telephone,

which he had apparently left on speaker. He leaned his palms on the desk and sighed. "Sorry, Mama."

Maddie hid a smile.

"Sounds like somebody's there with you," his mother said. "We'll talk later."

"No, it's all right." Hunched over the desk, Jake raised his eyes to Maddie's face and seemed to hesitate. "Finish telling me about the car."

Maddie wondered why he didn't tell his mother who was in the office with him. She'd met Mrs. Hopkins at Noah's funeral, at Rita's, and then three or four more times when Jake had been in the hospital and Maddie had attempted to visit him. It had been Jake's mother who had explained in the kindest way possible that her son didn't want to see anyone. So Maddie was no stranger to Jake's mother, and she was a little hurt that Jake hadn't given her an opportunity to say hello to the woman who had been like a second mother to Noah.

As Mrs. Hopkins described the problem she was having with her car's brakes, Maddie lifted her hand in a silent farewell to Jake and started to back away.

He widened his eyes at her and held up his index finger, signaling her to wait. "I don't want you driving it until I have a look," he said to his mother as he walked around to the front of the desk.

"I won't do any unnecessary driving," his mother said. "But I have that appointment with Dr. Huang tomorrow at four. I'll be extra careful."

"No," Jake said firmly. "I'll take you there. I was planning to do that, anyway, because I want to ask why he still hasn't changed your blood-pressure medication."

"All right, son. If you're sure."

"And about that other thing." Averting his face from Maddie, Jake rubbed the back of his neck. "Don't forget that I expect you to call me the very instant you hear anything. Good news or bad, Mama, you *call* me."

"I said I would." His mother's tone was placating.

It was none of Maddie's business, but Jake was clearly worried about something. She wouldn't ask about it, but she could definitely pray that whatever it was would turn out well for him and his mother.

"Since you're taking me to my appointment," Mrs. Hopkins said, "maybe we could have an early dinner at that new Japanese restaurant."

Jake raised his eyes to the ceiling and grimaced. He looked so much like a disgusted little boy that Maddie had to press her fingers over her lips to keep a giggle from escaping.

"Japanese food sounds just wonderful," he said in the same colorless tone in which he might have uttered, "I think I'm going to be sick." He closed his eyes. "I have to go, Mama." He waited for her to say goodbye, then leaned over his desk and ended the connection.

Maddie couldn't help chuckling. "Japanese food?"

Jake gave her a quelling look. "I detest Japanese food."

"And she hasn't picked up on that?"

"Oh, she knows." Jake's eyes followed Tripod as he hopped out of his chair and rubbed against Maddie's legs. "But she says it's healthy."

Maddie's grin faded. "It sounds like you're very good to her, Jake."

He shrugged. "She's my mama."

Noah had been the same way, Maddie thought as she bent down to gather Tripod in her arms. He'd never been ashamed of showing tenderness to his mama. As Maddie scratched behind Tripod's ears, she decided that was one of the most appealing qualities a man could possess. "I always liked your mother," she murmured.

"You've met her?"

Surprised, Maddie looked up. "Yes."

"At the funerals," he said as though realizing it for the first time. He'd been unable to attend either of them.

"At the hospital, too," Maddie said. "After they brought you back to Texas. I tried to visit you a few times, but…" She thought it wisest to abandon that sentence. She had never blamed Jake for declining her visits. He'd been in constant excruciating pain and he must also have been suffering tremendous emotional anguish.

He stared past Maddie's shoulder, his expression oddly bleak. "She was always there," he said softly.

"Jake?" It wasn't her business, but she couldn't help asking. "Is your mama…sick?"

"No," he said just a shade too emphatically. He closed his eyes. "No, she is not sick."

He seemed awfully desperate to believe that, but Maddie said nothing. She'd learned that pressing Jake to talk could have disastrous consequences.

He moved closer to Maddie and stroked Tripod's back. "This cat grows on people."

"Yes." Maddie tipped her head to look into Tripod's remarkably unattractive face. "What is it about him?"

"No idea," Jake said.

Maddie snuggled the animal closer. "I don't even like cats."

"Me, neither." Jake's voice had deepened, and its attractive timbre sent a frisson of pleasure through Maddie.

He moved closer. When Maddie looked up in confusion, she found his eyes narrowed and his brows drawn together, as though he was searching for the answer to a question that hadn't quite gelled in his mind.

He still hadn't given her any clue about why he had asked her to stay until he finished his phone call. Maybe the reason had slipped his mind. She didn't even consider asking, because Jake's moods were unpredictable, and she was still smarting from his last batch of hurtful words.

"I'd better let you get back to work," she said.

"I'll walk you out."

Jake waited while she returned Tripod to his favorite chair, then he accompanied her all the way to the front door. Maddie wanted to believe that meant he was reluctant to let her go, but she couldn't quite manage it.

Jake had never cared for heavy perfume on a woman, but unlike the other females of his acquaintance, Maddie didn't seem to bathe in the stuff. She just smelled good. He'd tried maneuvering closer to her, where he might haul in a good sniff and identify the subtle fragrance, but she had taken her leave before he'd been able to accomplish that.

Even now, as he watched her SUV pull away from the curb and blend into the light traffic on Veterans Boulevard, his mind couldn't stop searching for the answer. What was that comforting, familiar scent that made him want to lock her in his arms and press his face against her hair and inhale until his lungs burst? It was so fresh, so sweet. It was…

Baby shampoo.

He was surprised he'd been able to identify it. Surely it had been decades since he'd smelled baby shampoo. But maybe like crayons and cotton candy, it was one of those childhood smells you just never forgot.

What kind of woman used baby shampoo? The *young* kind, obviously.

Shaking his head, Jake closed the front door and headed back to his office. He wasn't sure how it had happened, but Maddie had sneaked past his defenses and burrowed under his skin. He knew very well what Noah would say about that: You shouldn't have *let* her.

But it hadn't been a question of his letting her. Maddie on a mission was almost unstoppable.

He met his partner in the hall. Travis opened his mouth to speak, but closed it fast enough when Jake glared at him. Resenting the knowing look edged with pity that Travis gave him in response, Jake strode into his office and slammed the door.

Late on Thursday evening Maddie sat at a deserted table in the dining facility across from the hospital eating a bland chicken-salad sandwich and watery vegetable soup because she was too hungry and too tired to get up and get something else. She had just finished a twelve-hour shift and was looking forward to hitting her bunk just as soon as she put this food in her belly.

"Hey, Mad." Lt. Wayne Pepper, a tall, husky blond nurse who had recently left the OB floor of the hospital and was now working in the neonatal-intensive-care unit, slid his tray onto the table and sat down next to her. "Mind some company?"

"Not at all, Wayne." She smiled pleasantly, even though she hated being called Mad. It sounded so…*angry*. But she'd never told him that because he was a nice guy and she didn't want to hurt his feelings. "How's life in the NICU?"

"I met Dr. Ice Princess today," he said.

Finished with her dinner, Maddie shoved her tray to one side and folded her arms on the table. "Who's that?"

"Dr. Nora Blake." Wayne's blue eyes narrowed as he pronounced the name. "Pediatric cardiologist. She's one of those doctors that shouldn't *be* a doctor."

Maddie had met Dr. Blake only a couple of times, but had been told by two other doctors and a fellow nurse that she was highly skilled. "That's not what I hear," she said mildly. "They say Dr. Blake is brilliant."

"That doesn't mean she cares."

"About the kids? I'm sure you're mistaken." It was true that Maddie had found Dr. Blake's demeanor cool and scrupulously professional. Yet Maddie had seen the woman warm up to Ali. "Some people just don't like showing their emotions," she said, thinking of Jake.

Wayne's broad shoulders lifted in a shrug. "Maybe she's okay. I guess not everyone can be as sweet as you, Mad." He stared at the two chili dogs on his plate. "How come the worst DFAC on post has to be the one right across from the hospital?"

"They do a good breakfast here," Maddie said. She didn't like the way everyone complained about the chow at the DFACs. The people who prepared it had feelings, and they were probably doing their best. It couldn't be easy feeding thousands upon thousands of soldiers three times a day.

"So says Maddie Sunshine." Wayne ruffled her hair, just as he might have a kid's.

That made her think. "Wayne, how old you think I am?"

"Uh…" He looked her up and down, clearly at a loss for words.

"I'm not fishing for compliments," she assured him. "I just need to know the truth."

His eyes narrowed on her face. "Twenty-three?"

She sighed. This was what she'd been afraid of: she looked even younger than she was. No wonder Jake still saw her as a kid. "Thank you," she said, belatedly remembering her manners.

Wayne shook his head, muttered, "Women," and bit into a chili dog.

Maddie slumped forward and rested her chin on the heel of her hand. How was she going to get home when she was too tired to walk out to her car? Just for a moment she allowed her eyelids to fall.

"You still house hunting?" Wayne asked.

She opened her eyes. "Yes, and I have a hot prospect. Last night I saw a place I loved, but it was beyond my budget. This morning the owner said we might be able to work something out, but it could be a week or two before he decides. So I'm just praying and trying to be patient."

Wayne nodded. "Hope it works out for you, Mad."

She yawned. "Thank you."

For a minute they both watched the national news on one of the big-screen TVs across the room. Then Wayne spoke without looking at her. "Hey, Mad? You know those two missing soldiers, the husband and wife who were all over CNN?"

Maddie bolted upright, suddenly wide awake. "Has there been a report?"

Wayne turned to look at her. "No, they're still missing."

Maddie slumped again.

"Mad, somebody told me they were friends of yours."

"They are," she said, emphasizing the present tense. "Whitney is my best friend."

Wayne put his arm around her shoulders. "Baby, why didn't you *say* something?"

Looking down at the table, she spoke with difficulty. "Because nobody believes they're coming back."

Wayne squeezed her to him. "I'm so sorry."

He talked as though they were dead. She was sick of hearing everyone talk that way. Maddie pushed Wayne's big arm away, shoved her chair back and got to her feet. Exhausted, full of bad food and on the verge of tears, she had to get out of here before she collapsed in a miserable little heap.

"Whitney and John will be found alive!" she insisted through her tears to a stunned-looking Wayne. She snatched up her tray and left him sitting there with his mouth hanging open.

Whitney was coming back.

She *was*.

As the beautiful notes of Brahms's *Lullaby* echoed down the halls of the maternity ward late on Friday afternoon, Maddie laid a newborn baby girl in her father's arms, then turned to make the baby's mother more comfortable.

"Ma'am?" The huge, ashen-faced sergeant looked down at the baby he held so awkwardly in his bulgy arms. "Is...is she all right?"

"Perfectly all right," Maddie responded as she draped a hot blanket over the trembling, exhausted new mama and tucked it around her.

"But she's all wrinkly. And her face is red. Ma'am, would

you please *look* at her?" In the exhausted man's distress, his voice had risen in pitch. "Is she all right?"

Maddie shared an amused glance with Myrna. Two days ago, this strong man had been in a Middle East desert barking orders at his squad. But in the unfamiliar environment of the hospital delivery room, his square jaw had gone slack with fear and the blond lashes under his round hazel eyes had become spiky from tears. He'd been terrified for his young wife, whose labor had been induced so that she could deliver during his two-week leave, and the poor man's last nerve had snapped when the baby in his arms had begun a lusty wailing.

Maddie addressed the new father in a crisp tone she hoped would help him get a grip. "Sergeant, that is a perfectly beautiful baby with a good, healthy set of lungs. Do you want her or not?"

"Yes, ma'am, I want her," the soldier said, pulling the baby closer to his chest in a protective gesture that squeezed Maddie's heart. "I most *definitely* want her."

This was the kind of nursing she had been made for, Maddie reflected as she watched the sergeant surrender his heart to his tiny daughter. This wasn't what she had set out to do; she supposed she would always be disappointed that she didn't have the strength to be a hero. But not every army nurse was cut out for that. Some were made to do this quieter work.

The Bible said people were gifted in different ways. Maybe she ought to try harder to be grateful for the gifts she had and stop wishing for gifts that had been given to others.

"I'm trying, Lord," she said under her breath.

The remainder of her shift was slow and uneventful. When it ended, Maddie went down to the NICU and sought out Wayne Pepper to offer an apology for the way she'd spoken to him last night.

"It's understandable, Mad," he said, watching her with compassionate blue eyes. "I hope you know I didn't mean to hurt you."

"I know that, Wayne. Thanks." She gave him a quick hug and then jokingly admonished him to stop slacking and get back to work.

She grabbed some dinner at the DFAC, then drove to Prairie Springs for another curbside look at the house she hoped might soon be hers. She wanted to see what it looked like in the dark and was disappointed to find it…*dark.* No lights had been left burning inside or outside the vacant house. She could barely even see it from the street.

Disappointed, she decided to give herself a different kind of treat. It was almost ten o'clock, closing time at the Creamery, but if she hurried, she might be able to purchase the last ice-cream cone of the evening.

The closest parking space she could find was almost a block away. She hustled down the sidewalk, past a man sitting alone on a bench next to the store's entrance. He was tucked back in a deep shadow, so she wouldn't have recognized him if she hadn't noticed the cane propped against the end of the bench. She stopped and turned, a little hurt that he would have let her pass him without so much as a greeting.

"Jake?"

"Hello, Madeline." The voice that came out of the shadows was as deep and velvety as the night. Had it held a note of resignation, or had she just imagined that?

She hesitated. If she went inside to get ice cream, would he be gone by the time she got back?

Probably.

She sat down beside him. "It's a nice night."

"Mmm-hmm." He stuck out his tongue and expertly turned his waffle cone as he took a long swipe of ice cream.

Maddie couldn't think of anything to say. He was clearly determined to avoid a romantic relationship with her, and she was trying to accept that. But he was rejecting her friendship, too. And *that,* she couldn't accept. Not when she knew his history. He was a wounded warrior and he needed her help, whether he believed that or not.

"Aren't you getting any?" Jake asked.

"Yes, in a minute." As Maddie spoke, the lights went out inside the store.

Jake glanced over his shoulder, then silently offered his own ice cream to Maddie.

She was faintly shocked. Licking somebody else's ice-cream cone seemed as intimate as a kiss. But she didn't want to offend him—and it wasn't as though she'd have minded kissing him— so she accepted the cone.

"Mmm," she said after an experimental lick. "Peaches and cream. Mr. Hopkins, you have impeccable taste."

"I like to think so."

Maddie took a few more licks, then handed the cone back to Jake and waited to see what he would do.

With perfect equanimity, he licked it.

"You seem awfully mellow tonight," Maddie ventured.

"It's a nice night." He was silent for a moment, then he added, "And I guess I'm celebrating."

"What are you celebrating?"

Another silence. For a minute she thought he wasn't going to answer, but then he said, "The lump in my mama's breast was benign. She finally got the biopsy results this afternoon." His voice dropped. "We'd been sweating that."

So that was the news he and his mother had been waiting to hear. No wonder Jake had been so upset when Maddie asked if Mrs. Hopkins was sick.

"That's a wonderful answer to prayer," Maddie said. "I didn't know exactly what to ask for, so I just prayed that all would be well with your mama."

Jake was still for a long moment, then whispered, "Thank you."

Without thinking, Maddie leaned her head against his shoulder. An instant later she realized what she'd done and froze. But Jake didn't seem to mind. At least, he didn't shrink away from her. So Maddie stayed right where she was and asked, "Wouldn't you rather be celebrating in Austin?"

"Just came from there. I took her back to that Japanese restaurant."

Maddie lifted her head and grinned at him. "Japanese food twice in one week? Poor Jake!"

"You said it." He licked his ice cream.

She didn't know how long his laid-back mood would last, so she was determined not to waste a moment of it. Returning her head to his shoulder, she enjoyed the crisp feel of his dress shirt against her cheek. She loved the comforting warmth that radiated from him. But it was his faintly spicy scent that comforted her the most. She closed her eyes and inhaled deeply.

A laughing couple walked past on the sidewalk. In the street a car horn tooted. But back here in the shadows with Jake, Maddie felt apart from the world, as though the night had wrapped its warm, protective cloak around the two of them.

She knew it wasn't going to happen, but for a few moments she imagined what it would feel like to be even closer to Jake. She pictured him turning his head and tucking a finger under her chin and lifting her face, then settling his warm lips against her mouth.

A loud crunch startled her out of her reverie. Jake had eaten most of his ice cream and was now disposing of the waffle cone in big noisy bites.

Certain that he would bring this strange and wonderful interlude to an end the second he finished his treat, Maddie saved him the trouble and sat up. She moved away a little so he wouldn't feel crowded, and then she sighed quietly. "I should be on my way."

Jake nodded and took another bite of his cone.

She stood. "I'm glad about your mother."

He nodded again.

Maddie had been excited tonight when she'd left the post, but now as she walked back to her car, she became aware of a crushing loneliness.

It wasn't an unfamiliar feeling. Sometimes at night she would awaken in the dark and recall a dream so good that its sweetness clung to her even after she became fully alert. But the harder she tried to recapture those images, the faster and farther they receded, until they disappeared altogether, leaving her bereft.

Back there with Jake, she had dreamed something beautiful. But she knew better than to reach for it, because it was already fading.

Chapter Six

Saturday dawned gray and threatened to deliver scattered showers. Maddie was hardly surprised that of the twelve people from Prairie Springs Christian Church who had signed up to go tubing on the Guadalupe River, only three girls, all college students home for the weekend, had assembled in the church parking lot.

She'd met the girls only once before. All three were tall, slim and quite beautiful. Kerry was a California blond, Angie was a gorgeous redhead, and Melissa had lovely long, black hair and enormous gray eyes. They were all very sweet, but from what Maddie had been hearing for the past ten minutes, all they could talk about was clothes and cute boys.

Good thing Travis was providing her with some adult company for this trip, Maddie thought wryly.

"We can leave as soon as my friend gets here," she said. Almost certain she'd felt a drop of moisture on her bare arm, she raised her face to the overcast sky. "But are y'all sure this is a good idea?"

Nobody answered. Maddie looked back at the girls and found all three staring past her in openmouthed astonishment.

"Who is *that?*" Angie breathed.

Maddie almost laughed. "That," she said without turning to look, "is Travis Wylie."

"Wow." Melissa's pretty dark eyes glowed with feminine interest.

Kerry tittered. "Maddie, you're the luckiest woman in the world!"

"No, I'm not. I mean, he and I aren't—"

"Hey, darlin'." Travis swept off his biscuit-colored hat and ducked to kiss her cheek. "Sorry I'm late."

Maddie didn't know what to make of the overly familiar greeting until she caught the mischievous twinkle in Travis's blue eyes. Obviously he'd overheard that "luckiest woman in the world" comment.

Maddie made the introductions, and after a brief discussion the college girls set out in one car while Maddie and Travis followed in his Range Rover.

"I saw Gloria at church the other night," Maddie said as Travis eased his truck onto Veterans Boulevard. "When I mentioned we were going tubing, she said I should tease you about being rich. She said it keeps you humble."

From under his hat, Travis slanted her an amused look. "Oh, don't worry about me. Jake keeps me plenty humble."

"And you return the favor, I have no doubt."

A dimple worked in Travis's cheek. "You're just about as quick as a hiccup, aren't you?" He shrugged. "Of course I return the favor. What are friends for?"

Maddie settled more comfortably in her seat, enjoying the

feel of the butter-soft leather and its pleasant smell. "Have you known him long?"

"Just since law school. We were study partners. We had something in common, both of us bein' older than most of the students and havin' already lived some life."

"What did you do before law school?"

"Helped run the family spread down in Uvalde. I went away to college and ended up back on the ranch, but my heart wasn't in it. I wanted to study law, and it took a few years before my daddy stopped seein' that as an insult to him. I'm not proud to say I resented Jake at first because *his* daddy, Connor, all but held Jake's hand and walked him to school."

That didn't sound like Jake. He'd never been the kind to hang back when he wanted something. Maddie stared at Travis. "Are you saying Jake didn't want to go?"

"Law school was Connor's idea," Travis said flatly. "All through the first year, Jake made noises about dropping out. He could do the work—he just didn't care about it. But Connor wouldn't let him quit."

"Why not?"

Travis glanced at her, his expression grave. He didn't answer right away, but looked back at the road and seemed to search for just the right words. "All Jake's dreams had been smashed to bits," he said slowly. "He had nothin' left. No passion. So until he found a new passion, Connor shared *his*."

Travis glanced over his left shoulder, then signaled and passed a slow-moving car. "I didn't understand that at first. I thought Connor was like *my* father, intendin' to keep his son on a short leash. But Jake wasn't fightin' Connor. Jake was fightin' *life*. Connor was just tryin' to channel all that angry energy into something productive."

Jake was still fighting, Maddie realized. At his father's prompting he'd begun a new career, but he was still struggling to find his place in a world where he could no longer live out his old dreams.

"It sounds like you've been a good friend to Jake," Maddie said when she was finally able to trust her voice.

Travis shrugged. "That road runs both ways."

For a few minutes Maddie said nothing, just stared through the windshield at the yellow and white lines disappearing under the Range Rover's hood. Then she turned to Travis. "Does Jake like being an attorney?"

"Oh, yeah. And he's very good. But the law will always be second best to Jake." Travis frowned at the road and appeared to think better about what he'd just said. "That's just an impression I've picked up. But with Jake, impressions are about all you have to go on."

"I know what you mean." Jake wasn't an easy man to read, and getting him to talk was next to impossible. But Maddie was determined to find a way.

By the time the tubing party arrived at the parking lot of the river outfitters' concession, several small patches of blue sky were visible between the clouds. Maddie and the girls changed into their swimsuits and pulled on rubber-bottomed river shoes to protect their feet from sharp rocks and stray pieces of broken glass. In the meantime, Travis rented a big black inner tube for each of them, plus an extra, to which he strapped a cooler filled with drinks and snacks.

To protect her pale shoulders, Maddie had pulled a yellow T-shirt on over her swimsuit. She rubbed some waterproof sunscreen on her arms and legs and face, then picked up a tube and carried it to the river's edge, where she dropped it onto the water with a satisfying splat. She stepped into the river, the cold water just covering her knees, and flopped into the tube. Spread out like a turtle on its back, she used her arms and legs to paddle to the middle of the narrow river, where she surrendered to the current.

Travis and the girls joined her, and their little flotilla was on its way. The spring-fed river was freezing, but after a few minutes the sun made a surprise appearance and everyone was comfortable.

Travis's idea of river wear was a pair of jeans and a cowboy hat. He looked adorable, and the girls could hardly take their eyes off him, but he stuck close to Maddie. She enjoyed his company, but she also wanted to hear more about Jake.

"Does he ever talk to you about what happened to him and my brother?" she asked.

"No." Travis cupped his hands and splashed water on his sun-dried shoulders. "Never."

That hurt. Maddie straightened her legs, lifting her feet out of the water, and pretended to study the bright yellow-and-aqua mesh tops of her river shoes. Just as she'd suspected, Jake was doing nothing to keep Noah's memory alive.

Travis snaked out a long arm and pulled Maddie's tube next to his. Then he leaned toward her, looking serious. "What do you know about post-traumatic stress disorder?"

She dropped her feet back into the water and stared at her companion. "Are you talking about Jake?"

He looked over his shoulder as though assuring himself they weren't being overheard and then he nodded.

She wasn't certain why the question surprised her. Even heroes like Jake could suffer from PTSD. She'd seen that with her own eyes. But she had also seen the prejudice. Many people thought the condition evidenced a weak mind or even cowardice. "PTSD is nothing to be ashamed of," she said crisply. "It doesn't mean a person is—"

"I know that." Travis almost growled the words.

"I'm sorry. It's just that there's still a lot of ignorance about PTSD. Few people realize that over thirty percent of soldiers who see combat are going to end up suffering from some form of depression, anxiety or post-traumatic stress. But what makes you think—"

"He has flashbacks."

Maddie stared. "He told you that?"

"No. He won't admit it. But I've seen it. He gets a look on his face that sends chills up your spine, and you know he's somewhere else. It lasts for a few seconds and then he kind of shakes himself and goes on like nothin' happened, and you wonder if you just imagined the whole thing."

Heartsick, Maddie asked, "How often does it happen?"

"I can't say. I see it maybe once a month. I've asked him about it, naturally, but he flat denies anything's wrong. Always says he's just tired. I never gave it much thought until lately. If I'd been shot out of the sky like he was, I'd be havin' nightmares in the daytime, too." His voice deepened with almost palpable concern. "But it's gettin' worse."

"Why do you say that?"

Travis tipped his head back slightly, and even though his eyes were deeply shaded by the brim of his hat, Maddie read concern in them. "This past week it happened twice. I mean, I *saw* it twice. And since I don't follow him around day and night, you have to wonder…" Travis left that sentence dangling. "Anyway, he seemed more…disturbed than ever before. There were even tears in his eyes."

Maddie hoped Travis was mistaken, but she had a bad feeling that he wasn't. Poor Jake. Hadn't he been through enough?

Behind them, one of the girls shrieked. Maddie and Travis both whipped around to see what was wrong. The girls were just having a splash fight, so Maddie beamed an indulgent smile at them and resettled in her tube.

"Don't y'all lose my Dr Pepper out of that cooler!" Travis called to them in a teasing tone. When he turned back to Maddie, his smile was gone. "You're a nurse. You could broach the subject."

No, she couldn't. Maddie sighed deeply. "He won't talk to me, Travis. Not about anything that matters."

"I guess I'm not surprised." Travis flipped his hands in the water and splashed his chest. "Jake's never been much of a talker."

But he *had* been once. Like Noah, he'd been full of plans and enthusiasm and his love of flying—and he had talked about all of it. Turning that over in her mind, Maddie realized that just because Jake and Travis enjoyed a cordial working relationship, it didn't necessarily follow that they would share their innermost secrets and fears. "Do you know if there's some other friend he might…"

"Jake doesn't *talk*," Travis said almost harshly. "Ever. To anybody. I've been to dinner at his mama's house a few times, and she's let some things slip. That's how I knew about your brother. But Jake doesn't talk."

And that was the worst thing he could do, bottle up his feelings and pretend he was fine.

Maddie had a niggling thought that she was guilty of the same thing, but she pushed it aside. Her problem was nothing next to Jake's. She might be faking happiness, but she fully expected to recover what she had lost. It wasn't the same thing at all.

"I'm gonna crash y'all's private party," red-headed Angie trilled as she paddled toward them.

"Guess I'm putting a damper on your social life," Maddie said in an amused undertone to Travis.

"Those chatterboxes?" His blue eyes widened in amazement. "Maddie, they're babies."

She took another look at the girls and guessed they must all be around twenty. She supposed they were a little young for Travis, and that made her think about the thirteen-year age difference between her and Jake. If she had just met him, she might have persuaded him that it didn't matter. But they *hadn't* just met, and she suspected Jake couldn't look at her without remembering what she'd looked like with braces on her teeth.

"What are y'all talking about?" Angie asked as her tube bumped Travis's.

"Serious things," Maddie said, smiling at her. "And we shouldn't be doing that on a day like this, should we?"

Travis brought his hands together with a loud clap. "Okay, let's party." He looked over his shoulder at the two other girls, who had charge of the cooler. "Kerry, why don't y'all come over here and share that food?"

They opened canned soft drinks and enjoyed a picnic lunch as they continued to float downstream. The girls giggled and flirted shamelessly with Travis, and Maddie realized just how young they were. Five or six years ago, she had been where they were now, with nothing more on her mind than her nursing classes and what she was going to wear for her date on Saturday night. But since that time, she'd finished nursing school in Dallas, joined the army, taken a sixteen-week emergency-nursing course at Walter Reed in Washington, been deployed to the Middle East and come back to Texas to learn a new specialty.

She was no kid, and it irked her that Jake thought otherwise.

"Hey, Travis, want me to rub some sunscreen on your shoulders?" Kerry shook back her wet blond hair and held up a tube of cream, her eyes hopeful.

"Nah. I never burn."

Maddie looked him over. "Your shoulders are getting a little pink," she said doubtfully.

"It'll turn to tan. I spend every weekend outside." He held out a thoroughly bronzed forearm for her inspection. Melissa grabbed it and exclaimed over its hardness. As Travis gently shook her off, he turned to Maddie with an amused look that said he'd told her so; the girls were babies.

Just like she was to Jake.

On Monday morning Jake met with a painfully young army aviator who was about to be deployed to the Middle East and who needed a will drawn up. Warrant Officer Charles W. Brown had been aptly named, Jake decided as he contemplated the spherical head under the guy's close-cropped blond hair. Brown was twenty-two years old, he had announced proudly, the youngest Apache pilot in his battalion.

Twenty-two? He didn't look old enough to be shaving, let alone piloting an Apache gunship. But that was the army's business, not Jake's.

The kid was nervous. He sat in Tripod's chair, both knees

jiggling, and he kept rubbing his palms on the pants of his uniform, probably to wipe off sweat. If the thought of making a will got him this wound up, how would he conduct himself in a firefight?

Don't go there, Hopkins. Get your mind back on business.

Tripod rubbed against Jake's right leg. Jake nudged him away, hoping he'd go back to his favorite chair and make a new friend.

He did. He hopped up and settled across the pilot's lap.

The knee-jiggling stopped. "Uh…" The startled pilot rubbed a hand over his round head and appealed to Jake. "I don't like cats."

Jake shrugged. "Me, neither."

Warrant Officer Brown gave Tripod a couple of awkward pats. "This is the ugliest animal I have ever seen."

Tripod yawned and made himself more comfortable.

"If we might continue…" Jake picked up his ballpoint pen. "In the event of your death, how would you like your property distributed?"

The pilot stroked Tripod's back and answered that question and all that followed with perfect composure. Busy congratulating himself on his successful experiment in cat therapy, Jake was blindsided when Warrant Officer Brown asked if Jake had ever served in the military.

Jake couldn't lie about a thing like that, but neither was he willing to discuss it, especially not with an Apache pilot. "I was in the army," he admitted, and then he discouraged further questions by adding tersely, "A long time ago."

After Tripod's new friend departed, Jake wandered over to his office window. Staring almost unseeing at the massive crape myrtle that dominated his front yard, he was barely aware of its purple-flowered spikes bobbing in the light breeze. Without volition he recalled the days when he had been just like Warrant Officer Charles Brown: young and strong and confident, eager to take on the world.

Jake, too, had been unnerved by the process of making a will before leaving on his first deployment. He and Noah and the other pilots had dealt with their fears by swaggering and cracking morbid jokes that had seemed hilarious at the time but weren't remotely funny now. Several of those men had never come home.

It had been a mistake to allow his thoughts to go down that road, Jake realized as he began to feel a familiar prickling on the back of his neck. Once again, his mind was on the verge of unraveling.

Apaches were the toughest birds in the sky, designed to withstand heavy combat damage and still make it back to base. But Jake and Noah had just lost their wingman, and now their own ship was going down.

Their left engine was on fire and they were still being pummeled from all sides. Much more of this and their heavily armored crew compartment would be ripped open like a tin can—as had happened to the other Apache. Jake's tail rotor had sustained heavy damage and at fifty feet off the ground, he had almost no control over the aircraft.

"What have you got?" he shouted to Noah. The Apache systems were fully redundant; if the command pilot or his controls were disabled, the copilot/gunner could fly the bird home.

"I've got nothing." Noah sounded more bewildered than frightened as he stated the obvious. "We're done, Jake. We're going in."

"Hang on!" Jake yelled.

A scant three seconds later they hit the ground.

Jake winced as he felt the impact, and then suddenly the horrifying sounds and images were gone.

The purple blossoms of the crape myrtle bounced gently in response to a puff of wind. Through the open door of his office, Jake heard Gloria laugh, and then a phone rang. It was an ordinary Monday morning. While Jake's mind had been AWOL, the world had gone on without him.

With his left hand, he squeezed the back of his neck and willed his tension to let go. Maybe it was time to—

No. He gave his head a hard shake and returned to his desk. There was nothing remarkable about a soldier who broke into a cold sweat every time he recalled the carnage he'd witnessed and participated in. A soldier without a load of bad memories was a soldier who'd never seen any action. So there was nothing special about him. Nothing worth discussing with a shrink.

And he had work to do.

A few minutes later, his mind firmly back on business, Jake made his way down the hall to the conference room that doubled as his and Travis's law library. As he entered the room he was surprised to find his partner bent over the long table sorting some papers.

"Thought you were in court," Jake said.

"I was. Just got back."

Jake spotted the book he needed on a high shelf just behind Travis. It was a bit of a stretch, so he propped his cane against the bookcase and laid one hand on Travis's shoulder to aid his balance.

"Ow!" Travis cried, flinching from his touch. "Watch the sunburn."

Grabbing the edge of a shelf, Jake managed to steady himself. "Sunburn?" he asked as he again reached for the book.

"On my shoulders," Travis said.

With the heavy law book safely in hand, Jake retrieved his cane. "Wylie, you spend your weekends at the ranch. You're used to working in the sun."

"Not without a shirt." Travis gathered up some papers and rapped their bottom edges on the table to make a neat stack. "But I didn't go to the ranch this weekend. I went tubing on the Guad with some friends."

Tubing? Had Travis's 'friends' included a certain dark-haired army nurse with sweet blue eyes? Jake braced himself to hear the details, but none were forthcoming. Travis had turned his attention back to his papers.

Jake felt a muscle jump in his clenched jaw as he waited for his lowdown skunk of a best friend to stop pretending nonchalance. *"Well?"*

Travis raised his head and regarded Jake with cool blue eyes. "Somethin' on your mind, Hopalong?"

"You spent the day with her," Jake grated out, "and you weren't even planning to tell me about it."

Travis straightened to his full height, which put him about three inches above Jake. "When you gave me her phone number, you neglected to mention that I'd be required to file regular reports."

"Don't be ridiculous," Jake growled.

"I'm not the one who's bein' ridiculous." Travis drilled him with a look. "If you don't want her, Hopalong, why do you care who she goes out with?"

"I *don't* care. It's just that…" Jake stopped because he didn't have a clue how to finish that sentence.

"Yes?" Travis folded his arms and looked politely interested.

"Nothing." Jake tucked the law book under his arm and stormed back to his office.

His surly mood had blown itself out by the time he plopped into his desk chair. He had to admit it was unreasonable to object to Travis spending time with Maddie, especially when it had been *his* idea to begin with. It was just that…

Once again, he found himself unable to complete that thought. Disgusted, he opened the book he'd just fetched from the library. He found what he needed and skimmed a few pages, but his thoughts kept returning to Travis's sunburn.

It was odd that Maddie, who was always so eager to take care of people, hadn't insisted on protecting Travis's manly shoulders by slathering sunscreen all over them. But apparently she hadn't done that.

Jake didn't allow himself to wonder why that was such a comforting thought.

When her work schedule permitted, Maddie attended the Wednesday-night prayer service at Prairie Springs Christian Church. She'd found tonight's service particularly meaningful because several intercessory prayers had been offered regarding the safe return of Whitney and John Harpswell. Maddie had been greatly comforted by those reminders that God knew exactly where the couple was and that He was in control of their situation.

Prairie Springs was a wonderful town, full of good-hearted people. They had opened their arms and taken Maddie in, and she was profoundly grateful. She was ready to put down some roots, and Prairie Springs was the place she wanted to do that. Even if she got orders and the army shuttled her off somewhere else, this would be home, the place she'd come back to when she finished her service.

For three weeks she'd been combing the real-estate ads in the local paper. She was excited by the thought of moving out of her tiny quarters and into a house of her own, although she was determined to accept God's timing for that. For now, it felt good to make whatever plans she could and dream about the sunny future that must surely await her.

As the worshippers filed out of the church, Gloria Ridge caught Maddie's arm. From behind the glasses that magnified her kindly eyes, the older woman gazed at Maddie with motherly concern and said, "Olga Terenkov just told me you and Whitney Harpswell are best friends."

Gratified that Gloria had used the present tense, Maddie felt her bottom lip quiver. A jerky nod was the only answer she was capable of delivering.

"Oh, you poor thing!" Gloria hauled Maddie against her plump body for a lung-flattening hug. "You must be having an awful time!"

Drawing back, Maddie forced a wobbly smile. "I'm okay. There's always hope."

"There sure is," Leland Ridge chimed in. A long-limbed former rodeo cowboy, Gloria's husband had been one of the people who had prayed for Whitney during the service. "Honey, you just hold on to that."

"You're both so nice." Maddie didn't want these dear people worrying about her, so did her best to blink the moisture out of her eyes and brighten her smile.

"Well, you just remember—" Leland further endeared himself to Maddie by the awkward way he patted her shoulder "—you have friends right here."

As they descended the church's front steps together, Leland spoke over Maddie's head to his wife. "Does she know about Saturday?"

"Oh!" Gloria grasped Maddie's arm and pulled her close. "We want you to come to our barbecue on Saturday night. It's going to be a real, old-fashioned party. Leland's borrowing a great big smoker so we can have brisket and sausage and chicken."

"We're rentin' tables," Leland added as they all stopped at the bottom of the steps. "And Gloria's gonna make a whole washtub full of her famous potato salad."

Disappointment flooded Maddie's heart. "Thank you so much, but I can't. I'll be on duty at the hospital until midnight."

"Well, plans can change," Gloria said bracingly. "You just remember that the invitation stands. We'll start serving food around seven, but you'll be welcome any time." She squeezed Maddie's arm. "We live on William Travis Street, the very last house before the dead-end at the river."

"Next to the park?" The little picnic area on the Prairie Springs River had become Maddie's favorite spot to sit and think.

"No, the park's at the end of David Crockett Street," Leland said. "Although you can also get there from James Bowie Street. That's the one that forks off—"

"Travis, Crockett and Bowie?" Maddie was unable to suppress a smile. "Are you giving me driving directions or a history lesson on the fight for Texas's independence?"

Gloria chuckled appreciatively. Leland's weathered face hosted a brief smile, but then he turned serious.

"This is a town that appreciates heroes, Maddie. Not just

the dead ones, but the live ones across that river." He nodded in the direction of Fort Bonnell.

Noah had been a hero. And Jake. Both had been awarded medals for meritorious service and valor. But Maddie would never be a hero.

Sighing, Maddie pushed back some strands of hair the balmy evening breeze had blown across her cheek. Then she thanked Gloria and Leland and took her leave.

As she walked to her car, two more friends called to her from across the parking lot, wishing her a goodnight. She waved to them, the ache in her heart easing a bit.

She would never be a hero. But in her own small way, she could brighten the lives of the people around her. Between her work, her volunteer activities at Children of the Day and her involvement with her church family, just for starters, she had ample opportunities to bring good cheer to others. Someone with her special talents could build a satisfying life here in Prairie Springs, Texas.

And that was exactly what Maddie intended to do.

Chapter Seven

Jake needed some advice on a legal matter, so he had asked one of his father's old friends, an Austin attorney, for a consultation over dinner on Friday evening. When the man expressed a strong preference for Japanese food, Jake had held back a sigh and said he knew just the place.

It was nearing midnight when Jake headed back to Prairie Springs after an evening spent drinking hot tea and repressing shudders of revulsion as his father's friend gulped cold, quivering fish like an eager dolphin. He skipped the interstate in favor of the old hilly, curvy two-lane highway, which was much more fun to drive, particularly on a fine late-summer evening.

Because he'd eaten nothing at the restaurant, he stopped at the drive-through window of a small-town hamburger joint. Back on the deserted highway, he hadn't gone another two miles before he crested a hill and spotted the emergency flashers of a car on the road's shoulder. He decided to stop, if only to make sure the driver had a cell phone and had called for assistance. But as his foot touched the brake pedal, he noticed the vehicle was a yellow Ford Escape. Grimly, he pulled in behind it and turned on his own flashers.

Of course it was Maddie. She had her interior lights on, so Jake could see her clearly. As could anyone driving past— didn't she realize that? Did she believe that every man who pulled off the road when he saw a young woman alone was a *nice* man?

His temper smoldered as he approached her car. It burst into flame when he realized she was so absorbed in the booklet she was reading that she was completely unaware of his presence. Even worse, her window was rolled all the way down. Anybody could have reached in and—

He didn't allow himself to finish that thought. But neither did he attempt to check the fury in his tone when he said, "Good evening, Madeline."

"Oh!" Startled, she dropped the booklet on her lap. Then she recognized Jake and her face broke into a smile. "Jake! You're the answer to my prayers!"

He'd been called a lot of things in his life, but never the answer to a woman's prayers. In another time and place, that would have pulled a laugh out of him, but right now he was too angry. He glowered at Maddie and waited for an explanation.

"My headlights aren't working," she said. "I was driving along and suddenly they just went *off*. Scared me to death." She patted her chest as though to calm her racing heart, then picked up the booklet she'd dropped. "I've been looking at the manual, but I don't see anything about—"

"You've blown a fuse," Jake interrupted, perilously close to blowing a fuse of his own. Why was she on this road alone at this late hour?

She shook her head, rejecting his diagnosis. "No, my interior lights and the emergency flashers are working just fine."

"Because they're on a different circuit," Jake replied with a patience he was miles from feeling. He glanced over his shoulder as a car approached and zoomed past. At least Maddie had pulled all the way onto the road's shoulder, which was fully as wide as the traffic lanes.

"I carry spare fuses in my car," he said. "Call the auto club and tell them you won't be needing them, after all."

She gave him a blank look. "What auto club?"

He should have known. "You don't belong to the auto club?" Of course she didn't belong to the auto club. Why join the auto club when all she had to do in the event of a car emergency was wait patiently for a Good Samaritan to come along?

Jake pinched the bridge of his nose. A minute ago he'd thought he couldn't possibly be any angrier, but he'd been wrong about that. He longed to drag her out of her seat and shake some sense into her. A woman alone should never, *ever* rely on the kindness of strangers if she had to stop on a deserted highway at midnight.

But that was Maddie. Foolish, trusting Maddie.

"I've been thinking about joining," she said. "But look how God took care of me tonight. I prayed for help and you showed up five minutes later."

Her stubborn optimism was going to drive him insane. "And what if I hadn't shown up?" Not waiting for her answer because there was no earthly way she could answer that question to his satisfaction, Jake stalked back to his car.

He checked the toolbox he carried in the trunk. Sure enough, he had some extra fuses. This would be a quick fix, and then he and Maddie could go their separate ways.

He couldn't wait. After almost making a fool of himself over her at his office and then letting her snuggle against him outside the Creamery, he had renewed his resolve to avoid her company. He wasn't even planning to attend Gloria's barbecue tomorrow evening because he knew she would have invited Maddie.

Gloria adored Maddie. The whole town did. Madeline Bright was everyone's little ray of sunshine. There was nothing wrong with that, but life wasn't *all* sunbeams and rainbows, and Jake was in a position to know.

He trudged back to her car and opened her door. "I need to get under the dash."

"One second." She leaned to her right and pulled something out of the glove compartment. "Here's a flashlight," she chirped. She pressed the switch, not realizing that the light's business end was pointed straight at Jake's face. "Oops!" she said when she blinded him with the powerful beam. "Sorry."

As spots danced before his eyes, Jake stood back to let her out of the car. He needed to get at the fuse panel, which ought to be under the dash on the driver's side, but kneeling outside the car would be a tricky move with his weak leg. So he left Maddie's door open and walked around to the passenger side. Lying across both seats, he ducked his head under the steering wheel and located the fuse panel.

Maddie handed him the flashlight, then squatted beside the door opening and leaned in. Annoyed, Jake turned his head and opened his mouth to point out that she was crowding him. But their noses almost bumped and he found himself staring into her wide, curious eyes.

He had always feared that if he gazed at her lovely face for any longer than a couple of seconds, his eyes would get stuck on her. That was exactly what happened now. But then he caught a whiff of baby shampoo and remembered just in time that he had absolutely no business wondering if her pink mouth was as soft as it looked. Shutting his eyes briefly, he mentally poked a stick at his anger to get it stirred up again.

"What are you doing?" he asked in his frostiest tone.

"Watching." She pushed back the hair that had swung against her face. "So I'll be able to fix it next time."

"Well, you're in my light."

She moved, but only a little. "You're torturing me, you know."

Jake fumbled the flashlight. *He* was torturing *her?*

She picked up the flashlight and handed it back. "You've been eating french fries. I can smell them on you."

Jake clenched his jaw even tighter. "There's a bag in my car. Go help yourself." Maybe that would keep her away from him for a minute.

"You shouldn't eat while you're driving," she said. "It's not safe."

Not *safe?* Incredulous, Jake raised his head to glare at her, but she was gone.

"Not *safe,*" he grumbled as he popped the front panel off the little box next to the door frame. He'd found her alone by the side of the highway at midnight with her window rolled down and her interior lights on, paying absolutely no attention to what was going around her. And she had the nerve to tell *him* about safety?

He located the bad fuse and snapped it out. Another car whooshed by, rocking the SUV as Jake inserted the new fuse and replaced the cover on the box. He wriggled out the passenger door and retrieved his cane, then walked around the SUV's hood and met Maddie next to the driver's door, where she stood happily munching his fries.

He reached past her and turned on the headlights.

"I have lights!" She looked at Jake like he'd done something marvelous. "*Thank* you!"

"Any time," he said, hoping she heard the sarcasm in his voice. He leaned against her back door and looked up at the bright stars, wishing he could get as far away from Madeline Bright as they were.

"I took a bite of your cheeseburger," she burbled. "I smelled the onions and couldn't resist." Smiling impishly, she ate another french fry. "Okay, maybe it was *two* bites."

Jake's hand tightened on the crook of his cane. "Just hurry up and finish my dinner so you can get back on the road."

"Are you always this grumpy when you're hungry?" She poked a french fry at his mouth.

Jake parted his lips and accepted it without thinking because his gaze had just caught on her face again. In the glow from her interior lights, her skin was as milky white as the rising moon. Her eyes were shadowed and mysterious, tempting him to lean closer and learn their secrets. And then there were her softly parted lips…

Just in time, Jake heard a car approaching. He turned his head, glad for the interruption, but as the car came closer he sensed that something was wrong.

Unlike the other drivers who had seen the flashing lights and the parked cars and moved into the other lane, giving them a wide berth, this one roared past on the very edge of the road. Maddie squealed as Jake caught her around the middle and yanked her against him. The car passed a mere three feet from the end of her open door. And then they were alone again, wrapped in each other's arms beneath the night sky.

Jake's heart was beating double time, and his fear quickly flashed into anger. "What are you doing out here so late?" he demanded.

Maddie leaned her forehead against his chest. "I had to drive a friend to the airport in Austin."

"Why did you take this road?"

"The same reason *you* took it." She stepped back, out of his arms, which was just fine with him. "Because it's a fun drive."

"It's not a *safe* drive," Jake snapped. "Not for you. Not at this hour, alone." When she opened her mouth to reply, he shook his head. "Get in the car, Madeline. It's not a good idea for us to stand here like this."

Speeding cars weren't the only danger out here. Jake was desperate to get away from Maddie before he made the colossal mistake of kissing her.

Without another word, she got into the car. Jake closed her door and watched as she pulled the seat belt around herself and started the engine.

He knew his harsh words and manner had hurt her, but maybe that was a good thing. Sweet Maddie needed to learn she wasn't safe with him.

"Good night," she said, avoiding his eyes. "Thank you for fixing my lights."

"No problem," Jake replied, his tone softer now. But it *had* been a problem, and he hoped she understood that.

Back in the Beemer, he reached for his cheeseburger and was dismayed to find she had eaten almost all of it. "You said two bites!" he called after her as the taillights of her SUV disappeared over a hill.

The little scamp had made off with his french fries, too.

He just hoped that was all she intended to pilfer from him. He'd begun to suspect she might have some designs on his heart.

If she did, she was in for a fight. Jake's heart might be a scarred, shriveled, pathetic thing, but it was all he had left, and he'd die before he let any woman steal it.

Maddie glanced in her rearview mirror and saw Jake's BMW round a curve more than a quarter of a mile behind her. She was barely traveling at the speed limit, but although she'd been on the road for several minutes, he still hadn't caught up. That could mean only one thing.

She sighed. It was pretty sad when the object of your affections couldn't even stand to drive on the same road as you.

"Thanks a lot for that ego boost," she muttered to the headlights in her mirror.

She had a remarkable talent for bringing out the worst in Jake. And half the time, she didn't even know what she had said or done to set him off. Like tonight, for example. He'd been as grouchy as an old bear. What was his problem?

Part of it had undoubtedly been her own carelessness. Somehow she had allowed herself to get so distracted that she'd been completely unaware that he had pulled off the road and walked up to her car window. No doubt he'd imagined her being overpowered by a man with nefarious intentions. But she was usually more careful and besides, she wasn't helpless. She'd taken her first self-defense class while still in nursing school.

She had a feeling he'd been angry about something more than the bad judgment she'd demonstrated tonight, but she couldn't imagine what that might be.

She ate the last cold french fry and crumpled the empty bag in her fist. Why did everything have to be so complicated? If Jake wasn't looking for romance, couldn't they just be friends? He had to know she wasn't just going to walk away and forget him. Not when they shared so much history. Even apart from that embarrassing childhood crush, Jake had been almost as dear to her as her own brother—and her mama had loved Jake, too. Why was he so eager to forget all that?

Maddie believed that what Travis had witnessed must indeed have been flashbacks, so it seemed likely that Jake was suffering from post-traumatic stress disorder. Not that she was qualified to diagnose him, but she believed PTSD would explain Jake's reluctance to talk about Noah. PTSD sufferers often coped with the agony of their nightmares and flashbacks by suppressing their emotions—sometimes so effectively that they withdrew from the people they loved and needed most.

Since Jake denied having flashbacks, Maddie wondered if he suspected what he was dealing with and was attempting to "handle" it on his own.

It hurt to think of him fighting that battle all by himself, in secret. But how could anyone help and comfort a man who was so determinedly building walls around his heart?

There was nothing like a good old-fashioned Texas barbecue to lift a man's spirits. When Jake arrived at the Ridges' house at seven-thirty on Saturday night, the backyard was teeming with women in floral dresses and men in western shirts and neatly pressed, indigo-colored Wranglers. Little boys tugged on their sisters' ponytails and babies screamed for their mamas while country music blared loud enough to rattle the windows on the modest ranch-style house.

Long tables had been set up in rows and covered with mismatched cotton cloths, their edges fluttering in the light evening breeze. Most of the guests had already sat down to eat, and Jake was eager to join them. When Leland lifted the cover of the meat smoker, the tantalizing aromas of beef sausage, brisket and barbecued chicken made Jake salivate like a dog that hadn't eaten all week.

Jake had told Gloria he had other plans for tonight. But then he'd run into Leland this morning at the gas station. Excited about the barbecue, the old man had leaned against his pickup and mentioned several of the guests who were expected—and a certain army nurse who was not. And then Jake suddenly remembered that he was free tonight, after all.

He greeted several people, but made sure each hello moved him closer to the food table. When he finally reached it, Gloria tucked a napkin and some plastic cutlery into his shirt pocket while Leland handed him a plate of sliced brisket and beef sausage. Balancing his weight on his right leg, Jake hooked his cane over his wrist and spooned potato salad and pinto beans onto his plate.

"Hey, Hopalong. Thought you had other plans tonight."

Jake glanced over his shoulder at Travis. "Turned out I was free, after all."

Travis moved next to Jake and thrust his plate at their host. "How about givin' me some more of that fine sausage?"

Leland grabbed a pair of grilling tongs and turned back

to the smoker. "You boys seen that Help Wanted sign over at Jimmy Land's place?"

Jake looked a question at Travis.

"The old drive-in south of town," Travis explained. "Great cheeseburgers."

"That's the one." Leland returned Travis's plate with two big logs of sausage on it. "Ol' Jimmy stays open till two o'clock in the morning, and he's always had trouble findin' people who want to work that late. So he got one of them magnetic-letter signs and spelled out, 'Now hiring closers, $12 an hour.'" Leland slapped one of his rangy thighs and laughed.

Travis shook his head as he plopped a spoonful of potato salad onto his plate. "Why's that funny?"

The old cowboy pushed his hat back on his head and folded his arms "Well, sir, some smart-aleck kids keep stealin' the C off Jimmy's sign."

Travis grinned. "Uh-oh."

"You see the trouble," Leland said approvingly. "Poor Jimmy's been wearin' hisself out explainin' to everybody that whatever the sign says, he is *not* hirin' *losers* at twelve dollars an hour."

Jake chuckled appreciatively, but then he heard a ripple of feminine laughter that made his heart drop a couple of inches inside his chest.

"Guess I'll just stick with my nursing, then," came Maddie's amused voice. All smiles, she stepped forward to greet Leland and Travis, explaining that she'd been able to trade shifts with a friend. Then she turned to Jake, and both her smile and her voice went flat. "Jake," she said with the barest of nods.

"Hello, Madeline." He'd been pretty rough on her last

night, and from the look in her eyes she had decided to be annoyed about that, rather than hurt. As their gazes locked, she raised her chin a notch and Jake couldn't help admiring her spirit.

Leland gave Maddie's shoulder a fatherly pat and walked away to greet another friend.

Travis cleared his throat. "Y'all need me to excuse myself?"

"Yes," Maddie said determinedly, her eyes steady on Jake's.

"No," Jake said at the same instant.

"I need another Dr Pepper, anyway," Travis said. He turned one of his lady-killing smiles on Maddie and tipped his hat. "Real good to see you, darlin'."

She broke eye contact with Jake and touched Travis's sleeve. "We'll talk later," she said warmly.

Jake scowled at his partner.

"Just tell me one thing," Maddie said when they were alone. "If you had known I was going to be here, would you have stayed away?"

Jake met her gaze squarely. "Yes."

"I'm not stalking you, Jake." There was a defiant edge to her words. "These are *my* friends, too."

"I know that."

She stared at him for another moment, then her pale-yellow sundress swirled as she turned on her heel and strode away. Jake thought about following her to apologize, but what was the use?

The phone in his pocket vibrated. He checked his caller ID, then, noticing that Leland had returned to his station by the smoker, asked permission to go into the house to return the call in private.

"Go right ahead," Gloria answered, having overheard the

question as she cut into a giant sheet cake shaped like Texas and frosted to resemble the Lone Star flag. "And when you come back, bring the big dish of pickles I forgot. It's on the top shelf of the refrigerator."

Jake nodded, then set his untouched plate of food on the corner of a nearby table and headed for the house.

Inside, he settled on a chair at Gloria's cluttered kitchen table and placed his call. He quickly concluded his business, but was in no hurry to return to the party, not when Maddie was running loose out there in a pretty yellow dress, her dark hair spilling all over her shoulders.

Pulling out another chair and propping his left leg on it, he wondered how long he could reasonably hide here in the kitchen.

The screen door creaked, and when Jake turned to see who had come in, his evening was ruined all over again.

"So this is where you're hiding," Maddie said.

"I was just returning a phone call." Jake wished he didn't sound so defensive.

She pulled out a chair. "Jake, I want to apologize."

He was careful to avoid her eyes lest he be sucked into their blue depths as he had been a few minutes ago. "There's no need, Madeline."

"Apparently there *is*, because you can't even stand to look at me."

He had no idea how to respond to that, so he said nothing.

Instead of sitting down, Maddie pushed her chair against the table and squeezed its wood back until her knuckles turned white. "Would you tell me something honestly?"

His eyes shifted to her face, and she looked so lovely and vulnerable that he opened his mouth to say yes, he would tell her anything she wanted to know. But he quickly discarded that foolish notion and shut his mouth again. There were any number of things he couldn't tell her.

"Never mind," she said dully, turning away. "I'm sorry I bothered you."

"Madeline, wait," he said, but she kept going. As she grasped the door handle, something inside Jake broke loose.

"Maddie."

She stopped, and when she turned around, her bleak expression pulled Jake to his feet.

"It isn't true that I can't stand to look at you," he said. "In fact, I find you very…" He faltered, unnerved by the knowledge that he was about to give her more of the truth, more of himself, than he'd given anyone in a long time. "I'm very attracted to you," he said baldly. "So it's a bad idea for us to spend time together."

Why? The word wasn't audible, but he'd seen her mouth form it.

He shook his head at the ceiling. "Didn't your mother ever warn you about men like me? Didn't Noah?" He allowed her to see his frustration. "Maddie, I would *hurt* you."

"No." She walked over to him and reached up to lay her hand against his cheek. "You'd never do that, Jake."

He hardened his heart against the trusting look in her eyes. "Do you think I'd be satisfied with holding hands and stealing a few chaste kisses?"

"You don't mean…" She withdrew her hand and looked at him sideways. "You're not trying to tell me that you…"

"Think about you in a way I shouldn't? Yes, Madeline, that's what I'm trying to tell you."

Her eyelashes fluttered and her cheeks turned rosy as his

harsh words sank in. For a moment he thought that would be the end of the conversation, but he should have known better. This was *Maddie*. Tenacious, doggedly optimistic Maddie. And she was shaking her head.

"No," she said with quiet conviction. "You'd never hurt me, Jake."

"There's only one way to be sure of that. Leave me alone."

"I can't," she whispered.

Jake suddenly felt very old and tired. "Go back outside, Madeline." He closed his eyes briefly, which was a mistake, because while he wasn't looking, she wrapped her arms around his waist and leaned her head against his heart.

He stood stiffly, not returning the embrace and doing his best not to be moved by the comforting warmth of it. When she raised her head, he almost kissed her, but then she said something that startled his brain back to full alertness.

"I think I'm falling in love with you, Jake."

Almost roughly, he pushed her away. "Oh, no, you don't. If you're looking for a boyfriend, go find someone your own age."

Her bright blue eyes narrowed and drilled him like twin laser beams. "I'm twenty-six, Jake, not sixteen. So don't presume to tell me that what I'm feeling isn't real."

"I'm sure you believe it's real," he began in the conciliating tone he used to calm overwrought clients. "But these feelings—"

"*Stop* it," she commanded. "I know you don't care about me that way. But that doesn't—" She stopped and drew a ragged breath. "That doesn't change the way I feel."

She was angry. That was good. He'd much rather deal with a ticked-off Maddie than a lovesick one. "Okay, I'm sorry. I'm just trying to make you understand why it's not a good idea for us to be alone together."

"Oh, I understand." She propped her hands on her slim hips and gave him a haughty look that was completely at odds with her usual gentle demeanor. Maddie Bright was as sweet as sugar, but there was some spice in her, too. "You're afraid of me, aren't you, Jake? You're afraid of *feeling* something."

Afraid? His brain stumbled. "I'm not afraid of—"

"Prove it." She tipped her head back and stared defiantly into his eyes.

He sighed. "I'm not going to kiss you to prove a point, Madeline."

Just as she opened her mouth to argue, the screen door screeched. Maddie jumped guiltily away from Jake.

"I sent both of y'all after those pickles," Gloria scolded good-naturedly.

"Sorry," Maddie mumbled, ducking her head and blushing again. "I forgot."

"I'm sorry, too," Jake said, hoping to deflect Gloria's attention from Maddie's pink cheeks. "We just got to talking."

"Talking." Gloria chuckled as she opened the refrigerator. "Yeah, I saw that."

Behind Gloria's back, Maddie arched her eyebrows and aimed a look at Jake that clearly communicated her intention to finish their conversation when they were alone again. Jake shook his head. They would never *be* alone ever again. He'd make sure of that.

He hightailed it out of the kitchen before he could get into any more trouble. He did his best to mingle with the other party guests, but those awful words of Maddie's were playing on an endless loop in his head: *I think I'm falling in love with you, Jake.*

He'd give just about anything to talk to Noah right now. But Noah wasn't here, and whose fault was that?

Jake was no longer hungry, but he snatched a cookie off the dessert table. Standing alone near a speaker blaring country music, he didn't hear the pair of low-flying helicopters until he might almost have reached up and touched them. When he caught the birds in his peripheral vision, he quickly ducked his head and focused on his shoes, lest his mind come unhinged.

He wondered again why he had chosen to live on the doorstep of Fort Bonnell, a place that was full of helicopters and memories. It was at Fort Bonnell that he and Noah had been trained in air combat. So why had he come back here?

Travis had suggested setting up their law practice in a small town, but it had been Jake who'd decided on Prairie Springs. Even now, he couldn't be sure that his choice hadn't been based on a subconscious desire to punish himself.

As the Apaches thundered overhead, Jake bit into his cookie. It wasn't a plain sugar cookie, as he had assumed, but the taste was vaguely familiar.

With his mind full of Maddie and Noah and helicopters, it was a minute before Jake realized his mouth had begun to tingle as though from a series of tiny electrical shocks. Appalled, he stared at the cookie in his hand. He now knew beyond any doubt what flavor it was.

Peanut butter.

Chapter Eight

Like many of the other party guests, Maddie lifted her face skyward as two Apache gunships flew overhead, so close that the figures of the four crewmembers were easily discernible in the cockpits.

"Those boys are low enough to smell the barbecue!" Leland yelled over the cacophony of whining engines, whirling rotors and country music.

Maddie had never been able to look at an Apache without thinking of Noah and Jake, so even though she was angry with Jake at the moment, her gaze strayed in his direction. Her heart squeezed painfully as she noted that except for the muscle twitching in his jaw, he stood perfectly still and stared fixedly at his feet. Nearly all color had drained from his face.

Had the mere sight of two helicopters disturbed him to this degree?

Maddie advanced two steps and then hesitated. Why bother going over there? He would just reject her again. She was about to turn away when he suddenly opened his hand and dropped a cookie on the grass. For an instant his fingers remained splayed as though he'd been burned. Then he headed toward the house.

Hearing her name called, Maddie turned and smiled at Olga Terenkov, who wanted to know if Maddie had seen Ali in the past few days. Maddie found herself stammering her reply because something about Jake's behavior niggled at her mind. He'd looked stunned, almost as though he'd been stung by a wasp or…

Maddie finally pieced together what she had seen. Jake had been eating a cookie. And earlier, Maddie had noticed a plate of peanut-butter cookies on the dessert table.

She excused herself and raced after Jake, terrified that she'd find him in the throes of an anaphylactic episode, a serious allergic reaction that could be fatal within minutes.

She reached the kitchen door and wrenched it open just as Jake collapsed onto a chair. He let go of his cane, and as it clattered to the floor he leaned back and slid his hand into the pocket of his jeans.

"Oh, good." He wheezed as Maddie fell to her knees beside him. "It's you." His eyes closed briefly as he struggled for breath.

"Let me do it," Maddie said, reaching for the auto-injector he'd pulled from his pocket. It had to be jabbed into his lateral thigh muscle and was designed to go right through his jeans. She was worried he'd do it wrong and waste the dose of epinephrine he so desperately needed.

"I've done it before," he gasped as he removed the injector's safety cap and laid it on the table. In one quick, fluid movement, he jammed the injector into the side of his thigh. He held it there for several seconds, then removed it and massaged the injection site with his fingertips.

Maddie sprang up from her knees and grabbed the phone on the countertop. "Make sure it's empty," she couldn't help saying at she called 9-1-1.

Jake gave her a feeble smile. "I've done this…before," he reminded her, his chest heaving as he checked the syringe to make sure he'd completed the injection.

"Try to stay calm," Maddie said as she waited for a dispatcher to answer. "It'll be easier to breathe." When her call was answered, she confirmed the address and identified herself as a registered nurse, then explained that Jake was having a serious anaphylactic reaction.

"Do you have another dose?" she asked after she'd ended the call. The EMTs would almost certainly be here inside of ten minutes, but if something delayed them, Jake might need more epinephrine to keep his airway open.

When he shook his head, she wanted to snap at him that he needed to carry *two* doses. But this was hardly the time to point out that if the shot wore off and he needed another one, he could die before the ambulance arrived.

The screen door squeaked and Gloria stepped into the kitchen. "Are y'all okay? Olga said you both took off like—" Gloria broke off and stared at Jake, who was slumped in the chair, his arms resting on the table as he struggled to breathe.

"We have an emergency," Maddie said quietly.

Gloria winced as Jake fought to inhale. "Have you called 9-1-1?"

"They're on their way," Maddie said. "Gloria, it would help if you waited out front and directed them in here."

Clearly a woman who could be counted on in a crisis, Gloria nodded firmly. "I'll do that. And I'll be praying."

Maddie knew there were few things as terrifying as being

unable to breathe. She pulled out a chair so she could sit in front of Jake, her knees touching his. She grasped both his hands and caught his wide-eyed gaze, then took slow, even breaths, hoping he would try to match them.

There was no awkwardness between them now, no anger or misunderstanding. They were just two scared friends, holding on to each other.

"I'm…sorry," Jake whispered.

Hoping a little joke would help him relax, Maddie batted her eyelashes. "Sorry you didn't kiss me when you had the chance?"

He gave her the ghost of a smile.

It took every ounce of Maddie's will to hold on to her own smile as she prayed silently that help would come soon.

Chapter Nine

The emergency medical technicians asked dozens of questions, many of which Maddie was able to answer, taking some of the stress off Jake. By the time she climbed into the back of the ambulance to accompany him, the EMTs had already put an oxygen mask on him, started an IV and checked his blood pressure. Once the ambulance was on its way, they connected him to a heart monitor and clipped a sensor on his index finger to monitor his oxygen saturation. Finally he was given an aerosol breathing treatment through his oxygen mask.

After a couple of minutes Jake closed his eyes and sighed. Maddie sighed, too, knowing the crisis was over. She wiped tears from her face and offered a silent but heartfelt thanks to God.

At the hospital Jake was given an antihistamine and some cortisone, then he had an EKG to make sure he hadn't suffered a heart attack. Maddie went to call Gloria and give her a report. After that she returned to the patient room where Jake sat in a vinyl armchair looking a bit dazed but breathing normally.

"They want to observe me for at least four hours," he said.

Maddie had expected that. "Yes, that's standard for this kind of thing. But it's getting late, so I imagine they'll keep you overnight. That's what I told Gloria just now. If you'll give me your keys, I'll get them to Leland and then he and Gloria will swing by on their way to church in the morning and drop off your car. They'll bring your cane, too."

Jake avoided her eyes. "That would be good."

Without thinking, Maddie reached out to smooth his rumpled hair. "I could go downstairs and get you something to read."

He shied away from her touch. "No, thanks."

"Well, then, do you want me to—"

"Madeline," he interrupted, "I appreciate everything you've done."

That sounded like a dismissal. She'd been hoping he'd let her keep him company for a while, but that had been a foolish dream. Clearly he hadn't forgotten her rash disclosure that she was falling in love with him.

"Then I guess I'll be on my way." She wanted to kiss his cheek, but settled for laying her hand over his where it rested on the arm of the chair.

Once again he carefully withdrew, pulling his hand out from under hers. His rich brown eyes were full of apologies as he said, "Thanks again, Madeline."

She held back a sigh and started for the door. Halfway there, she turned. "I'm on duty at eight in the morning. I'll stop by before you leave."

"You don't have to bother," he said without expression. "I'll be fine."

She stared at the floor and nodded slowly, understanding that he was asking her to leave him alone.

She kept her back straight and her head high until she was out of his sight, but then her shoulders slumped, weighed down by the heaviness in her chest. She trudged to the hospital's front entrance and pushed through the glass doors. After grabbing a few deep breaths to steady herself, she used her cell phone to call a friend and ask for a ride to Gloria's so she could pick up her SUV. Then she settled down on a bench to wait.

Until the instant she'd so unwisely blurted that she was falling in love with Jake, she hadn't realized it. She wished now that she hadn't told him. He didn't want her as a girl-friend, but he needed her friendship, and she might have been allowed to give him that if she hadn't burdened him with the knowledge that she hoped for something more.

How could she have been so stupid?

The evening breeze had cooled; a storm was blowing in. As Maddie pushed back some wisps of hair the earth-scented breeze had blown across her eyes, she discovered that her face was wet with tears.

As the cockpit filled with smoke, Jake grabbed his M4 carbine and crawled out of his seat. Noah was dazed and moaning, so it took some doing to pull him out of the wreckage. With an arm around Noah's waist, Jake half-sup-ported and half-dragged him away just as fire flashed through the cockpit.

Noah pushed away from Jake to stand on his own. "I'm okay," he said, sounding far from it as they watched the fireball consume their Apache.

They'd gone down between two hills, where for the moment they were safe from the insurgents' fire. They put a little more distance between themselves and the flaming helicopter, then took stock of their situation.

"Our guys are south of here," Jake said, gesturing with his rifle in that direction. Before the ambush, the two Apaches had been escorting a convoy on the ground. "But—"

"We're cut off." Noah finished for him. He attempted to take another step but swayed on his feet.

Jake caught his arm and steadied him. "Easy there, bubba." Noah's shoulder was bleeding, but there was little point in stopping to examine the wound. For one thing, it was too dark to see much. For another, Jake was no medic. Besides, they needed to find some cover before the insurgents who had just shot them down came over the hill looking for them.

Jake peered into the darkness, searching for the irrigation ditch he'd spotted from the air. That might offer some tall reeds for cover. Holding Noah's arm, he moved cautiously forward.

"There's the ditch," he said after they'd gone a few yards. He squeezed Noah's arm to get his attention. "You doing okay?"

"I've been better." Noah turned toward Jake and fainted in his arms.

Jake sat up in the hospital bed and rubbed his eyes to erase the horrible images of the nightmare. Would these memories haunt him forever?

To slow his racing heart, he mentally paged through a catalogue of comforting thoughts: roaring waterfalls, starry summer nights, the Longhorns winning the National Championship…

Maddie.

All right. But only because he was desperate. For a few

moments he allowed himself to dwell on the slow unfurling of her smile and the way the blunt ends of her glossy dark hair curved against her shoulders. He contemplated her low, melodious laughter and her light, sweet scent. The softness of the hand she had laid over his.

After his mind recovered its equilibrium, Jake slept until the sun was well up and Gloria had arrived with his cane and his car keys.

"Thank the Lord you're okay." Gloria settled onto a chair like a plump nesting hen. "One of the guests brought those cookies and put them with the other desserts. I never saw them." Her gray curls bounced as she shook her head. "I'm so sorry, Jake. I never imagined anything like that could happen."

"It wasn't your fault." He yawned. "And I'm fine."

"You gave us such a fright." Gloria flattened a hand over her heart to suggest palpitations.

"It's over," Jake said. "Let's forget it."

"Forget it?" The bulgy, magnified eyes behind Gloria's glasses had grown wet. "I *care* about you, Jake."

"I care about you, too." He hadn't realized it until this moment. He didn't like being fussed over, but all things considered, Gloria was a woman of good sense and character.

Smiling, she opened her purse. The scent of spearmint chewing gum wafted through the room as she produced a wrinkled handkerchief and applied it to the teary corners of her eyes. "I'd better go. Leland's waiting downstairs, and we don't want to be late for church."

After she was gone Jake got dressed and then sat in the chair to put his shoes on. How many years had it been since he'd been to church? he wondered as he slid his right foot into a shoe and gathered up the laces. He longed to feel as peaceful and clean as he used to feel after Sunday-morning worship services, but those days were gone. Going to church now and rubbing shoulders with the faithful would feel dishonest. Jake didn't really believe in God anymore.

He had just picked up his other shoe when there was a light tap at the door and Maddie came in, morning-fresh and efficient in her green nurse's scrubs. Jake was a little surprised to see her after the way he'd treated her last night, but he was glad she'd come. He shouldn't have been glad, but there it was. A disciplined man might control his actions, but thoughts and feelings were a much more difficult proposition.

Because Jake *was* a disciplined man, he would never hurt Maddie. But she could hurt herself, and that was exactly what was going to happen if she didn't stop trying to untangle the barbed wire Jake had wrapped around his heart.

"I've been thinking about this, Jake, and I have something to say." Folding her arms and raising her chin, she gave him a mutinous look that was truly adorable. She was such a curious mixture of strength and vulnerability. "You don't have to worry about me repeating what I said to you last night at Gloria's," she continued. "You've made your position clear, and believe it or not, I have some pride."

"That was never in doubt," Jake murmured. She really was magnificent. It was a shame he could never tell her that.

"So we're just friends, and…" She stopped and shook her head. "No. We're not even *that,* are we? You don't like being reminded that we share some history. So I guess we're just acquaintances."

"I'm sorry." What else could he say?

She huffed impatiently and strode over to where he sat. Jake was vaguely alarmed, not guessing her intentions until she took possession of the shoe he'd forgotten he was still holding. When she knelt in front of him and reached for his left foot, he almost smiled. She was angry and hurt, but she was still determined to take care of him. That was Maddie.

"Now that we've got that settled…" she slipped the shoe onto Jake's foot and tugged at the laces. "I also came to tell you they brought Ali in last night."

"Ali? What for?"

"An upper respiratory infection. He should respond to the treatment, but this will delay his surgery." She tied a neat, businesslike bow and stood up. "I'm not sure how much he understands about what's going on, but when I saw him just now, he seemed depressed."

"I'm sorry to hear that." Jake had suffered a lot, but he hadn't exactly been innocent, so there had been a certain justice to that. But why was God—if there really *was* a God—heaping so many troubles on that innocent five-year-old kid?

"He admires you." Maddie moved back as Jake placed the tip of his cane on the floor and got to his feet. "So I thought you might stop and say hello before you leave this morning. He's in room 512."

"Sorry, but I can't do that." He snagged his car keys off the bedside table and dropped them into his pocket. "I need a shower and a shave, and then I have to hightail it to Austin for an after-church brunch with some of Mama's friends. I'm already running late." He wasn't looking forward to the brunch, but he'd promised to be there so his mama could show him off to her friends. "I could see Ali this afternoon, though."

"He'd like that." Maddie's voice had dropped almost to a whisper. And just before she turned to leave, Jake thought he saw the shimmer of tears in her indigo eyes.

"Maddie?" He couldn't stop himself. He couldn't let her go, not like this. When she turned in the doorway, he blurted, "I'm sorry about the way things—"

She silenced him by raising both hands, palms out. *"Don't."* She gave her head the tiniest shake and said, almost inaudibly, "Please don't."

And then she was gone.

Jake was aware of a crushing disappointment that she hadn't stayed to argue with him. Reason insisted that was a wise course; between them was a chasm that could never be bridged. Again and again, Jake had seen her reject that reality and struggle to make a connection with him. He had practically begged her to stop trying.

And now, finally, she had.

On her way back from a meal break, Maddie stopped to pick a bouquet of the black-eyed Susans that grew wild in an empty lot behind the hospital. Thinking Ali might enjoy the bright golden flowers, she arranged them in a plastic water pitcher and took them to his room. She found the little boy clutching a teddy bear and watching cartoons.

"Is he new?" Maddie asked, indicating the teddy bear, who wore boots and a cowboy hat.

Ali nodded listlessly. "He is Texas Bear. Grandpa gave him to me."

Maddie found room on a small table for her flowers, then she perched on the edge of the bed and studied the brave little boy she prayed for every night. In spite of all he'd been through—losing his parents, injury and illness, coming to a strange country—Ali had always managed to find a shy smile for everyone. As a nurse Maddie had witnessed the remarkable resiliency of children. But sometimes even a for-giving five-year-old's spirit could be crushed by adversity.

Maddie reached out and tugged on his earlobe, playing the little game he'd enjoyed during their interminable trip from the Middle East. He smiled, but his big brown eyes shimmered like dark pools of worry in his thin face.

Maddie tickled him under the chin. He giggled feebly and brushed her hand away.

What he needed was a long, healing sleep. "Let's turn off the TV so you can rest," Maddie suggested.

"Not yet."

Remembering a bit of silliness from her childhood, Maddie took two of the black-eyed Susans from the improvised vase and pinched off their stems. Closing her eyes, she tipped her head back slightly and placed the blooms on her eyelids.

As she'd hoped, Ali giggled at her new set of eyes: two big golden "irises" surrounding dark brown "pupils."

A low, masculine chuckle came from the direction of the doorway. "You used to do that when you were a kid."

Maddie tipped her head forward and caught a flower in each palm. Once again, Jake was seeing her as the child he'd known, rather than the woman she was. Hiding her despair, she nudged Ali with her elbow and smiled. "Howdy, Mr. Hopkins."

"Howdy, Mr. Hop-kins," Ali parroted in an exhausted little voice.

The boy was fading fast. Maddie was certain that if they left him alone now, he'd be asleep in mere moments.

"I'm sorry I couldn't come earlier," Jake said.

Maddie nodded. She could hardly fault a man for keeping a promise to his mama. "It was good of you to stop by," she said, laying her flower-eyes on the table, "but he needs to rest now." She reached for the TV's remote control and pressed the Off button.

When she looked down at Ali, his thick black lashes were already resting against his cheeks. She was about to rise from the bed when Ali's eyes popped open and he reached for her.

She stroked his short bristly hair. "Close your eyes, little one."

"My heart is sick," he fretted.

"I know, honey." She caressed his silky cheek with the backs of her fingers. "But Dr. Blake will make you all better, and soon you'll be able to run and play just like you did before. Everything's going to be fine." Aware that her voice shook a little on those last words, she brightened her smile and playfully tugged one of Ali's earlobes. "You go to sleep now."

His eyelids fell again.

Maddie remained for another moment, praying silently. Then she wiped the moisture from her eyes and glanced at her watch.

It was time to get back to work.

In the hallway, Jake fumed over what he had just seen and heard. As a nurse Maddie should have known better than to allow herself to become emotionally involved with Ali Willis. Yes, the kid was cute. But his upcoming heart surgery was extremely risky. Knowing that, Maddie should have held something back.

But no, that wasn't her way. Maddie gave all of herself, just handed over her heart to anyone who would take it, leaving herself open to all kinds of devastation.

When she stepped out into the hall, Jake gave her a piece of his mind. "You shouldn't have said all that."

She blinked at him. "All what?"

Her confusion underscored Jake's point and fuelled his irritation. "Madeline, there's a good chance that boy will die," he said bluntly.

She looked shocked. "There's every reason to hope that—"

"Hope is fine," he interrupted. "But you shouldn't make promises you can't keep."

"I didn't do that." She started walking toward the elevators.

Jake followed. "You told him everything would be all right."

She rounded on him. "Oh, give me a break. I was trying to comfort a five-year-old boy. Did you expect me to add a legal disclaimer to that?" She snorted and started walking again. "'Results described may not be typical for all patients,'" she mimicked.

Jake just shook his head. Attempting to ease the boy's fears was one thing, but Maddie was fooling herself. "Not everyone is 'fine,'" Jake insisted as they reached the elevator lobby. How a registered nurse, especially one who had seen the carnage wrought by men during combat, could stubbornly persist in believing life was all sunshine and roses was simply beyond his comprehension.

Maddie's eyes sparked with anger as she pressed the button to summon a car, but she said nothing.

Jake couldn't leave it alone. "Not everyone gets a happy ending, Madeline. Cute little boys and good men die every day. Remember Noah?"

"I'm not the one who has forgotten Noah," she said with quiet dignity. Then she turned to face the elevators, giving Jake her back.

As her shocked, angry silence roared in his ears, Jake

wished he hadn't gone so far. But the woman made him crazy. She persisted in spreading out her heart like a picnic blanket, never stopping to consider that it might get trampled.

He had tried not to care. He had tried not to notice her at all. But he could shut his eyes and cover his ears, and awareness of Maddie would just seep through his pores.

The rigid line of her back began to curve. When Jake saw her head droop and her shoulders roll forward, he pictured her bright blue eyes flooding with tears.

A better man would have apologized then and there. But Jake was too frustrated to risk opening his mouth again.

A bell sounded and the light on the elevator's call button went out, signaling the arrival of a car. Both Maddie and Jake were going down, she to the OB floor and he to the ground floor, but Jake figured she wouldn't want to ride with him. "I'll take the next one," he muttered, retreating a few steps.

He didn't allow himself to look, but when he heard the elevator door swish open he knew exactly what Maddie was doing: lifting her chin, squaring her shoulders and stepping forward like the brave soldier she was.

When another elevator arrived two minutes later, Jake followed her example.

Jake had promised Anna he'd drop by her office when he had time to discuss an immigration issue that had arisen for one of her war refugees. Late on Tuesday afternoon he found himself with a free hour and a desire to stretch his legs, so he walked the three blocks from his office to the graceful Victorian house that served as headquarters for Children of the Day.

As he approached the house, he noticed Maddie's SUV parked in front of it. His step faltered, but he reminded himself he was going to have to face her at some point; he had an apology to tender for his boorish behavior on Sunday afternoon. He still didn't know what had gotten into him, talking to her that way.

He had just started up the porch steps when Maddie blew out the front door and streaked past him like a comet. Instinct told him something was terribly wrong—and for once, it had nothing to do with him. She'd rushed past him without so much as a glance in his direction.

"Madeline?" Concern and confusion had robbed his voice of power, so he caught a breath and produced something close to a shout. "Maddie!"

"Let her go, Jake." The screen door opened again and Anna stepped out onto the porch, her eyes full of compassion. "Maddie just had some very upsetting news."

"What upsetting news?" Jake's gut knotted as he watched Maddie throw herself into her SUV. He hoped nothing had happened to her mother. Marva Bright had always been good to Jake, but he hadn't been able to face Maddie *or* Marva after Noah's death, not when he was the cause of their grief.

Pushing back a section of blond hair that had escaped from the silver clasp she always wore, Anna sighed. "My contacts in the area where Whitney and John disappeared say there's no hope. The fighting's worsened, and two soldiers alone couldn't possibly—"

"Who are Whitney and John?" Jake interrupted, his eyes on Maddie. He winced as she pulled out in front of another car, which managed to stop just in time. The offended driver laid on his horn as the yellow Ford roared down the street.

Waiting for an answer, Jake turned back to Anna.

"Don't you know?" she asked, frowning. "Whitney is Maddie's best friend. They grew up together in Dallas."

The name was familiar, but Jake couldn't put a face to it.

"Whitney married John Harpswell just recently," Anna said. "They were both army, in the same unit, and they were deployed to the Middle East. Several weeks ago they were part of a small convoy that was attacked. Everyone was killed, and the convoy was looted. But Whitney and John weren't found among the dead, and the insurgents weren't bragging about having captured two American soldiers. It doesn't look good."

No, it didn't.

"Maddie was holding out hope that they'd somehow escaped," Anna continued. But it's been almost two months now and…" Anna broke off and shrugged eloquently.

They couldn't have lasted. Not alone. That was what Anna was implying.

Why hadn't Maddie told him about Whitney and John?

He knew why, and he was so ashamed he could hardly breathe. He'd been growling at her like an injured wolf every time she reached out to him. When, exactly, could she have told him that her friends were MIA? And what indication had he ever given that he would care?

Jake slumped against the porch railing, his stomach churning. "How long has Maddie known about this?"

"They've been missing since the end of July. Maddie didn't know until earlier this month. I think a mutual friend told her the day after she arrived in Prairie Springs."

Jake closed his eyes and slowly shook his head, pitying the soldiers' families and friends—and most of all, Maddie. In that harsh, volatile region, anyone missing for that length of time was never going to be found. Not alive.

"Anna, do you know where she went?"

"No idea. But I'm worried. I've never known her to drive recklessly."

"It's not like her," Jake agreed. "She always thinks of other people before herself."

"Sometimes she goes to that little park on the river," came a voice from the doorway. "You might try there."

Jake turned to see Anna's mother, Olga Terenkov, studying him with sympathy. He didn't know why. *His* wasn't the heart that was breaking right now.

"Mother, she won't want anybody," Anna said. "You know Maddie isn't a person who shares her sorrows."

But that was exactly what she'd tried to do with Jake. She'd wanted to talk about Noah.

And he had refused.

Olga's eyes remained steady on Jake's. "Go after her."

"Mother, she wouldn't even let me put my arms around her." Anna's tone held an uncharacteristic note of impatience that Jake ascribed to worry. "You saw the way she took off. She doesn't want anybody right now."

"Sometimes what a person wants and what she needs are two different things," Olga said, still looking at Jake. "If she's not at the park, try the church. She doesn't think her apartment is very homey, so I doubt she'll run there to cry."

Jake hesitated. Olga loved matchmaking and had repeatedly mentioned Maddie to Jake in that context. But she also ran the grief-counseling center at Prairie Springs Christian Church, and Jake had a feeling she was now speaking in that capacity, rather than as a meddling friend.

He nodded his thanks, then turned to Anna. "I'll get back to you later on that immigration thing."

He hurried home to get his car. By the time he reached the park next to the river, Maddie was nowhere in sight. Jake drove to her church, but didn't see the yellow SUV on the street or in the parking lot.

For more than half an hour, he cruised through town searching for her. He tried repeatedly to call her, but she wasn't answering her phone.

Where did she go when she was hurting? Who did she turn to? Maddie was always helping other people, cheering them up, taking care of them.

But who took care of Maddie?

Chapter Ten

"No, Mama, nothing's wrong." Less than thirty seconds into their conversation, Maddie regretted giving in to the impulse to phone her mother. "I was just thinking about you and wanted to tell you that I love you."

Squirming on her rock-hard sofa to find a more comfortable position, Maddie realized that what she needed was a hug. Dallas was only a couple of hours away; she might have driven home if she didn't have to work tonight. But it was better this way, because one look at her puffy eyes and her mother would know she'd been crying.

"I love you, too," her mother said. "Are you sure everything's all right?"

Maddie had been deeply depressed since her awful encounter with Jake on Sunday, so when Anna told her about that phone conversation with one of her contacts in the Middle East, Maddie's self-control had simply shattered. She'd run out on Anna, brushed past Olga and nearly knocked poor Jake off the stairs as she fled. By the time she'd reached the main gate at Fort Bonnell, she'd been producing tears so copiously that the guard had suggested she pull off the road for safety's sake.

Now she smiled, hoping that would brighten her voice. "I'm just fine, Mama."

Have you been keeping Mama cheered up, Maddie-bird?

It wasn't that their mother had ever been weak. But when Noah had gone off to West Point, he'd worried about her adjusting to his absence. He'd been just fourteen when his and Maddie's father had died, so he'd had to grow up fast. But as conscientious and loving as Noah had been, he never realized what a heavy burden he'd placed on his five-year-old sister by extracting her promise to keep their mama happy.

Maddie had finally begun to understand all that, but the habit of hiding her feelings and putting on a happy face for the sake of others was so deeply ingrained that she didn't think she would ever break it.

"Have you heard anything about Whitney?" her mother asked.

As always, Maddie was prepared for the question and gave her stock answer. "There's still hope, Mama."

That was the truth. No bodies had been found, and that meant there was still hope.

Her mother sighed. "It's been such a long time."

Maddie closed her eyes tightly and gathered her strength. "I know, Mama, but there's always hope."

"Of course there is." Her mother paused. "I was thinking about Jake this morning. Is he doing okay after that scare on Saturday night?"

"Yes, he—" Maddie stopped and blinked in confusion. "How did you hear about that?"

"Hmm? Oh, you must have told me. Where else would I have heard about it?"

"He's fine. But, Mama, this is getting spooky. This is the second time you've mentioned something about Jake that I'm sure I never told you."

"You just forgot," her mother said reasonably.

Maddie gave up trying to get comfortable on the sofa and moved to the upholstered chair next to it. It was equally hard, no doubt because it had been designed by the same sadists who made the sofa. She sighed.

"You sound tired," her mother said.

"I am." She was tired of hiding her emotions and pretending everything was just fine. Tired of feeling like a failure because she couldn't cut it as an emergency/trauma nurse in a war zone. Tired of worrying about Whitney and John and sweet little Ali. Tired of constantly arguing with Jake, who desperately needed help coming to terms with all that had happened since his helicopter had been shot down.

She had never been more tired in her life, she realized as she pushed herself out of the awful chair and went to the kitchen to heat some water for a cup of tea.

"Take a nap before you go on duty," her mother advised. "Are you expecting any babies tonight?"

"There's always one or two. Did I tell you that every time a baby is born, we play Brahms's *Lullaby* over the PA system? Several of the nurses are Christians, and we have a pact to say silent prayers for the babies whenever we hear the music. That's not always possible when we're working, but if we're walking down the hall or on break or something, we always pray."

"That's sweet."

Maddie nodded as she set a mug of water in her microscopic microwave oven. Those daily opportunities to celebrate life were the best part of her new job. "This is a good place for me," she said. "It's a good hospital, Mama, and I love the work. And Prairie Springs is a wonderful town."

"When you find a house, I'll take a couple of days off work and help you get settled."

"I'd appreciate that."

"We could plant some pink roses in Whitney's memory. Remember how that girl always loved my pink roses?"

Loved. Past tense. Even her mother thought Whitney was dead. Tears filled Maddie's eyes as her heart cried out against the unbelief that surrounded her on every side.

It was hard to hold on to hope when she was the only one still making the effort.

Jake had worked through lunch on Wednesday, so late in the afternoon he strolled across the street to Coffee Break, where he bought a double espresso and a bag of his favorite oatmeal-raisin cookies. Finding the hip coffee bar nearly deserted, he snagged a wooden chair to use as a footrest and settled into a bulky club chair next to a window. He had always enjoyed the ambience of this place; in addition to the comforting aroma of freshly ground coffee beans, he found the hum of conversation and the occasional grinding and hissing of the espresso machines against a background of mellow jazz surprisingly relaxing.

As he bit into a cookie, he heard Maddie's voice. He turned in his chair and there she was at the counter, ordering a chai tea and trading pleasant remarks with the barista. Relieved to note that she seemed herself again, Jake snorted softly, for once amused rather than exasperated that their paths had crossed.

He considered and discarded a plan that called for him to sit very still and hope she would leave without spotting him. If they were both going to live in this town, it would be nice to do so peaceably. So when she got her tea and turned to leave, Jake extended an olive branch.

"Hello, Madeline."

She stiffened, then turned slowly, wearing a cautious look that made Jake feel like the kind of man who pulled wings off butterflies and knocked down kids' sand castles. With the barest of smiles, she nodded. "Hello, Jake."

She was a good fifteen feet away, but he held out his white bakery bag. "Oatmeal cookie?"

She shook her head and continued to eye him warily.

Jake smiled some encouragement at her.

She walked over and sat in the chair next to his and took a sip of her tea, watching him over the rim of the paper cup. No doubt she was wondering who this pleasant man was and what he had done with grumpy Jake Hopkins.

"I looked for you yesterday," he said. "I looked all over town."

Her eyebrows rose. "Why?"

Good question. He pushed a hand through his hair and thought about it, then shared his unedited conclusion. "To make sure you were all right." He paused. "*Are* you all right?"

"I'm fine." She stared down at her cup and tapped her short, neat fingernails against it.

"Why didn't you tell me about Whitney and her husband?"

Maddie looked up, startled. "You don't know them, Jake."

So she thought he wouldn't care? After the way he'd been

treating her, that shouldn't have come as a surprise. Still, something deep inside him began to ache. "They're people who matter to you," he said. "You've been worried about them. You might have mentioned that."

"What would that have accomplished, except to make you feel bad for my sake? You couldn't have done anything for Whitney and John."

"No," he agreed, swirling the coffee in his cup. "But I might have done something for *you*." Just for starters, he'd have been less critical of her. More patient, more understanding. And he'd have made sure she knew she wasn't alone.

"I've never dumped my troubles on my friends," she said diffidently. "I try to make other people happy, not add to their burdens."

Jake pulled his left leg off the extra chair and shifted so he could face her and make something very clear. "Nobody's happy all the time," he said gently "And nobody expects *you* to be. It's not wrong to share your troubles with your friends, Maddie. You could have talked to Anna or Olga, instead of trying to carry this all by yourself. You could even have talked to me."

She tilted her head and looked at him from under her raised eyebrows. "Is that why you tried to find me yesterday? Because you heard I was upset about Whitney and John and you wanted to…share my troubles?"

Jake nodded, hoping she wouldn't read too much into that. It was friendly concern, nothing more. Anna or Olga had been just as worried as Jake, and they'd have gone looking for her if he hadn't.

"You think I should have told you about Whitney," she said slowly.

"Yes." Jake nodded, beaming approval at her while silently congratulating himself on facilitating this breakthrough.

"I see. But just to clarify…"

She was struggling, really working for it, but she was getting there. Feeling proud of himself, Jake took a swig of coffee.

"You think it would be good for me to talk about my feelings," Maddie said.

Jake opened his mouth to say yes, that was it, she needed to talk. But the words died on his lips as he noticed the disquieting gleam lighting her blue eyes.

"All right," she said with a hint of asperity that worried Jake. "Here's what I don't get. If talking would be good for *me,* why wouldn't it be good for *you?*" Her hair swung softly as she shook her head, her eyes steady on his. "I'm not the only one who's been trying to go it alone, Jake."

Whoa. She'd broadsided him with that shot. Jake sipped his espresso, stalling, but his surrender was inevitable. "Okay," he said finally. If she needed this so badly, he'd give it to her, whatever the cost. "We'll talk about Noah."

Maddie had just won their battle of wills, but gloating wasn't her way. The bluebonnet eyes that searched his face were full of compassion. "Why is that so hard for you?"

He just looked at her.

"Why?" she asked again.

"Because I…" His lips worked, but he was unable to produce any more sounds. He fought the familiar, insistent tug on his mind, but in the end reality was wrenched from his grasp.

Noah had passed out again. Jake knew they couldn't stay hidden in the ditch, their lower bodies submerged in cold water, for much longer. Noah's breathing was labored, and when Jake felt for his pulse, he found the side of Noah's neck sticky with blood.

They'd waded into the canal to hide behind a stand of reeds after a burst of fire from an AK-47 had whizzed past their heads. Jake didn't think they'd been spotted, because they hadn't been fired on again, but it was impossible to be certain.

Four Apaches had just arrived and were asserting their authority with devastating thoroughness. The earth shook as another Hellfire missile exploded nearby, boosting Jake's confidence that the battle would be over in a matter of minutes. It could still be a while, though, before he and Noah were rescued.

Noah urgently needed a medic, and Jake was determined to get him to one. If he had to walk a mile with Noah draped across his shoulders, he'd find the strength somewhere.

He dragged his friend's limp body out of the water. His plan was a risky one, but Noah could die while they awaited rescue in the ditch.

Unfortunately there was no way Jake could run with Noah on his back, both of them bulked up and weighed down with body armor. Jake was doing well to put one foot in front of the other, so he prayed that the bad guys would be too busy with the Apaches to notice one desperate soldier cresting a small hill with his buddy on his back.

His prayers went unanswered. A burst of automatic-weapon fire ripped Noah's body out of his arms, then blasted Jake's legs out from under him.

"Jake?"

He slowly became aware of Maddie gripping his hand.

"Jake, your *face*…"

He reclaimed his hand before she remarked on the way it was trembling. "I'm fine." He took a long drink of coffee.

"Jake, did you just have a flashback?"

"No," he said swiftly. "No, nothing like that." He shook his head for emphasis. He could hardly tell her the truth when she sat there biting her bottom lip, her pretty eyes wide and worried. Besides, he didn't have *real* flashbacks. He wasn't one of those guys who heard a car backfire and then dived under a table and whimpered while clutching a mop handle he believed was an assault rifle.

No. He didn't have flashbacks. He just had…intrusive memories. Yes, that was it. He just had bad memories at inconvenient times.

Maddie's gaze hadn't left his face. "Tell me something. Do you ever feel guilty because you came home and Noah didn't?"

He couldn't think how to avoid giving a truthful answer to that question, so he indicated a reluctant affirmative by bowing his head.

"That's survivor's guilt," she said. "You must know that's common among soldiers who have lost friends in battle."

He knew that. But sometimes the survivors really were guilty.

"Major Carter told Mama and me the whole story," Maddie said. "You and Noah went down fighting, and then you tried to save Noah's life. Major Carter told us how brave you both were."

"Major Carter wasn't there," Jake said dully.

Maddie made an impatient noise in the back of her throat. "Jake, there's no reason for you to feel guilty just because—"

"I *am* guilty," he said harshly. "If you knew the whole story, you'd realize that."

She put her cup on the table next to her. "Then tell me the whole story," she urged in a tortured whisper.

No. It wouldn't be fair, unburdening himself to Maddie. As much as he ached for forgiveness, he couldn't do that to her.

"*Tell* me, Jake."

His heart sank as he realized she had already seen and heard too much to be put off. He gulped the rest of his coffee, but found no courage at the bottom of his cup.

Maddie took the empty cup from his still-unsteady fingers and set it on the table with hers. She also took the bag of cookies, which he'd been crushing in his other hand. Then she shifted in her chair, angling her body toward his, and waited.

Jake's gaze drifted past her shoulder. "It was a small convoy. They had to move at night, but it was just a short hop, and they didn't expect any trouble. They asked for an escort of two Apaches."

He swallowed hard and continued. "You probably know that Apaches are hard to kill. They're heavily armored, and they have redundant systems. But we were ambushed by a large band of insurgents with some enormous firepower, and our wingman went down like a ton of bricks." He gripped the arms of his chair and squeezed his eyes shut as pain blazed through him. "Jase and Brent were good men. Jase had been teaching Noah how to play chess. Brent had just become a father."

Hearing Maddie draw an unsteady breath, Jake let go of the chair's arms and curled his hands into fists. He couldn't do this. He couldn't tell her this. Not sweet Maddie.

"And then you and Noah were shot down," she prompted.

He nodded and opened his eyes. "We crawled out of the wreckage and took cover in an irrigation ditch. Noah had caught some shrapnel and was slipping in and out of consciousness. We were…" Jake trailed off and gave Maddie a pleading look. She couldn't possibly want to hear this.

"Go on," she said.

He swallowed again. "We were between two hills, caught in the middle of a firestorm. It went on right over our heads. It was…bad."

He condensed the story, sparing her as many of the awful details as he could. "We didn't know which side would come for us first, so we hid behind some reeds in a ditch. It was good cover. I knew our guys would get to us eventually, but I was worried about Noah, so I decided to—" He broke off and shuddered violently. If only he had made a different decision that night, Noah might still be alive.

"Major Carter told us you were seen carrying Noah on your back," Maddie said.

"That was my mistake. I couldn't tell how badly he was hurt, and I was…afraid. All I could think about was getting him to a medic."

Maddie's eyes had filled with tears. "Go on."

Jake ground his teeth. How could he have made such a bad call? "I should have *waited*," he said fiercely.

"You didn't know how long Noah could afford to wait," Maddie reminded him.

"No," Jake admitted, and then his mind was hijacked once again.

Dragging his useless legs behind him, Jake crawled over to Noah. He felt no fear or physical pain as he laid his head on his dead friend's chest. All he knew was a terrible sense of guilt and loss.

They should have stayed in the ditch, under cover. Help would have come eventually. Jake was no medic; maybe

Noah's condition hadn't been as serious as he'd assumed. Jake had been afraid, plain and simple. He'd surrendered to his fear and made a decision that had cost Noah's life.

And probably his own, as well. As he lay against Noah, he prayed that God would take care of his parents and Rita. He prayed for Noah's family, too.

His last conscious thought was of Noah's adoring little sister. Maddie was going to take this hard.

"Jake, you weren't responsible for what happened to Noah." Maddie's voice penetrated the darkness and pulled him back from the edge of insanity. "You had reason to believe he might not last until you were rescued. With the information you had, you made the right choice."

No. *No.* It was wrong. Jake shook his head. "The ditch was *cover.* Noah died because I tried to carry him over that hill." He pressed his fingertips against his eyelids until he saw red splotches. "What was I thinking?"

"You were thinking Noah's best chance was for you to carry him to safety rather than let him die waiting to be rescued," Maddie said firmly.

She still didn't understand. "I felt the rounds hit his body," Jake said savagely. "The impact jerked him out of my arms."

Maddie winced and looked away.

Despair slid through Jake as he realized what a horrifyingly graphic picture he'd just painted for her. "I'm sorry. I shouldn't have told you that."

She met his gaze. "You're forgetting that I've been over there."

No, he hadn't forgotten. It was just that he still had trouble picturing softhearted, innocent Maddie nursing wounded soldiers.

"Jake?" Her voice was no longer steady. "D-did he… linger?"

"No, it was quick." That was the truth, and Jake was glad to be able to offer that small comfort. "He was gone before I got to him."

"That must have been hard."

She had no idea. Grieving a friend's death was a simple thing; it just plain *hurt*. But knowing you had helped cause that death was something else entirely.

"Our guys saw the whole thing," Jake said. "I lost consciousness, but they said it was just a matter of minutes before they were able to advance and recover us." To stop his hands from trembling, he squeezed them into fists. "But Noah was already gone."

A tear tumbled down Maddie's pale cheek. She made no move to stop it. "What do you remember after that?"

Pain. Blinding, deafening, mind-paralyzing pain. But not in his legs. They'd given him drugs for that. It was the mental anguish that had made him beg God to end it all. He had known he'd never fly again, never walk again. But worse than any of that had been the knowledge that he'd gotten his best friend killed.

"I don't remember much of anything," he said. That wasn't remotely true, but the things he remembered were too ugly to share with Maddie.

"You had your first surgery at the CSH," she said, using the acronym for combat support hospital. "They got you stabilized and then put you on a MedEvac flight to Germany, where you had more surgery. When your parents learned it might be a week before you were sent on to Walter Reed, they got on a plane to Germany."

"Yes." He knew all that, not that he actually remembered much beyond the red haze of pain pierced repeatedly by shafts of sorrow and guilt.

Maddie's mouth thinned to a disapproving line. "But Rita couldn't be bothered."

Jake's impulse was to defend his wife, but he was distracted by Maddie's quiet outrage. "How do you know about that?" he asked.

"Mama pumped everyone for information about you. Doctors, nurses, your commanding officer. And your mother, of course."

Jake's face must have betrayed his confusion, because Maddie gave him an exasperated look.

"We were *worried,* Jake. Did you think we stopped caring about you after Noah was gone? We didn't. And we never understood why Rita didn't fly to Germany with your parents."

Rita had never liked flying, but that wasn't the only reason she hadn't rushed to his bedside. She and Jake had been more or less estranged since he'd left on that last deployment. Jake had hoped to patch things up when he got home—he'd done it before. But lying in the hospital bed, he'd let go of that hope and everything else. He'd just wanted to die.

In time he'd stopped praying for that.

And then he'd stopped praying altogether.

"Why did you never come see us?" Maddie asked. "I mean, I understand why you couldn't come at first, but when you finally got out of the hospital, we thought…" Stopping as the barista approached, she averted her face, no doubt because she was reluctant to be seen with wet eyes. Jake had a sudden, irrational urge to gather her into his arms and press her against his chest and hide her there, protecting her from curious stares and all other hurts, great and small.

"Y'all need anything?" the barista asked pleasantly as she picked up their empty cups and polished the table's surface with a damp cloth.

"Same again for both of us, please." Jake was embarrassed by the sound of his voice; it was low and gravelly, full of emotion. When the young woman was out of earshot, he answered Maddie's question. "I knew you and your mama were devastated, but I had no comfort to give you. Also, I was terrified that you'd ask questions and get the truth out of me—and that would have only multiplied your grief. I couldn't risk letting you find out that Noah might have lived if only I hadn't…"

"We wouldn't have blamed you, Jake." Maddie knuckled tears from the corners of her eyes. "How could we? Your only thought was to get Noah to safety. As far as Mama and I and the U.S. Army are concerned, you risked your own life to save him. It wasn't your fault he was beyond saving. God had other plans for Noah that night."

Behind the counter, an espresso machine rumbled and sputtered, sounding as though it was working as hard to make coffee as Jake's brain was working to make sense of Maddie's words. All these years, he'd believed his mistake had thwarted God's will for Noah. But Maddie spoke as though God had *intended* to take Noah on that awful night. Which suggested that even if Jake had made a different decision, the outcome would have been the same.

"I joined the army because of you," Maddie said. "Noah and those other two men couldn't have been saved, Jake, but *you* were saved, and I thanked God for the doctors and nurses who did that. I wanted to be like them. I wanted to work at a CSH and help save heroes like you." Her gaze dropped to her lap, where she twisted her fingers together. "But I don't have what it takes."

Another time Jake would have objected to being called a hero. But at the moment he was too puzzled by Maddie's suggestion that she had failed in some way. "But you went over there," he said. "You *did* it."

She gave him a crooked, self-deprecating smile. "It almost killed me. Whenever I could get away, I used to hide in one of the supply tents and cry."

And she thought that was something to be ashamed of? "Believe me, Maddie, there's nothing unusual about crying over injured or dead soldiers."

"It wasn't the crying. It was the *daily* crying. I just couldn't learn to compartmentalize things the way everyone else seemed to do." She shook her head. "I wasn't strong enough."

He couldn't believe she thought that. He curved his fingers under her chin and urged it upward, forcing her to lift her gaze from her restless hands and look at him. "You *are* strong, Maddie."

She tried to move her head to avoid his searching gaze, but he held her still. He wasn't going to let her get away with thinking she was some kind of failure. Not his Maddie.

"You didn't fail." Jake leaned closer and grazed her cheek with a butterfly-soft kiss. "You might have flooded the supply tent a time or two, but I know you did your job. So stop beating yourself up over the fact that your nature's not suited to nursing in a war zone."

She pulled in a ragged breath. "I know this is going to

sound silly when I say it out loud, but I had my heart set on being a hero."

Jake withdrew his hand and tried to work out her meaning. "Are you saying you believe what you're doing at Fort Bonnell is less *heroic* than what you were doing at the CSH?"

She looked surprised by the question. "Well, yes. Of course it is."

Jake couldn't agree. He remembered how Brent Ritchie, one of the pilots who'd died the same night as Noah, had broken down and cried after learning his wife had borne him a healthy son. The pregnancy had been high-risk, and Brent had been worried. But the doctors and nurses back home had taken good care of his wife and child. Jake was certain Brent had seen those people as heroes.

"Maddie, *all* nurses are heroes," Jake said. "None of you gets as much admiration as you deserve."

"Thank you for that." She gave him a watery smile, then leaned forward to blow her nose into a paper napkin.

Overcome by tenderness, Jake slid his hand under her silky hair and lightly massaged the back of her neck. Then the barista brought their drinks and Maddie smiled again and asked Jake if she could have a cookie.

For a few minutes they ate cookies and sipped their drinks in a companionable silence. Jake wondered if Maddie felt the way he did, but he didn't ask because he didn't know how to describe it. He just felt lighter, somehow.

Maybe it was better not to mention that. She might take it the wrong way and think he was open to a romantic relationship.

He wasn't. She might not blame him for Noah's death, but she was still too young, too innocent, too *special* for a man like him. He'd had his chance with Rita and he'd blown it. A man as selfish as he'd been didn't deserve another shot.

Reaching for his cane, he told Maddie he had to get back to the office. When he got to his feet and put some money on the table for the drinks, Maddie looked up and gave him a smile as fresh and sweet as a spring morning.

"Thank you, Jake. I think we both really needed this talk."

He felt a stirring of unease. "I'm glad we cleared the air, Madeline, but I don't think it would be wise to do this again. I don't want to hurt you, but…"

"I understand," she said softly.

The dewy look in her eyes told him another story. She *didn't* understand, not really, but Jake didn't know what he could do about that now. He made his way to the door.

Chapter Eleven

"Mama?" Twirling a damp, freshly shampooed lock of hair around her index finger, Maddie stared into the flame of the pillar candle that was currently providing the only light in her bedroom. "I'm sorry to call so late, but I've been meaning to ask you something, and I thought you might still be up."

Seated at the little desk, she tucked her feet up beside her and pulled the hem of her terry bathrobe over them for warmth. She'd been sitting in this chair thinking and praying for the past twenty minutes, but she hadn't yet found the answer she sought.

"What is it?" her mother asked.

Maddie knew this was a dangerous question to put to a mama who had recently begun making noises about grandchildren, but she didn't know where else to turn. "Now don't get all excited, because this is just a simple question," she said. "I don't mean anything by it. It's just something I've been wondering about, okay?"

"You want to know how to tell if you're in love," her mother guessed.

Maddie dropped the hair she'd been twirling. "How did you know?"

"When an unmarried woman tells her mama what you just told me, there's only one thing it *can* be." She paused. "Why do you ask? Is this about Ja—" She coughed. "Sorry. Had a frog in my throat. As I was saying, is this about any man in particular?"

Maddie's eyes narrowed. That cough had sounded as fake as a three-dollar bill. "Mama, you know I'm not even dating anyone right now."

"I know. I was just asking."

Yeah, right. Jake's name had almost tumbled out of her mama's mouth, and that spoke volumes about what was going on in her head. She had always adored Jake, and for that reason Maddie had been scrupulously careful during the past month to avoid talking about him lest her mama begin haunting bridal shops and drawing up guest lists.

"I'm twenty-six," Maddie reminded her mother, "and I've never asked you how you knew Daddy was the right man for you. I just thought it was something I ought to begin thinking about, that's all."

"Hmm," her mother said. "Well, as far as I know, there's only one foolproof test for determining—"

"There's a foolproof test?" That was precisely what Maddie had been hoping to hear. She glanced at the open spiral notebook on her desk and wondered if she ought to grab a pen. "What is it?"

"It's simple," her mama said. "When you find yourself thinking about a certain man all the time, consider *how* you're thinking about him. If you're all wrapped up in what he does for you and how he makes you feel, that's just infatuation. True love can *begin* with infatuation, but it's much more than that. You'll know it's true love when helping and supporting and making your man happy become driving forces in your life. You'll know it's true love when you find yourself thinking about his needs before your own."

After several seconds of dead air, Maddie realized her mother had finished. Conscious of a deep disappointment, she said, "That sounds a little one-sided."

"It isn't if the man loves you back. True love is a reciprocal relationship. You take care of him and he takes care of you. At least, that's how it worked with your daddy and me. We were happily married for over fifteen years."

Staring at the leaping shadows cast by the flickering candlelight on the white wall opposite her, Maddie nodded. "Thanks, Mama. I'll mull that over." She thought it prudent to add, "That way I'll be prepared when I find that special someone."

Her casual air seemed to do the trick. Her mother dropped the subject and asked about Maddie's classes.

"Taking classes online is more challenging than I expected," Maddie said. "But I'm doing well. Myrna, my preceptor, still hasn't really warmed up to me, but she's a good teacher, and that's the important thing."

They talked for another minute and then wished each other goodnight. After ending the call, Maddie sat for a long time watching the candle flame dance and thinking about Jake. Was she truly in love with him? She was afraid to examine her feelings too closely because Jake didn't love her and she didn't know if he ever could.

But she had a new question. Did true love have to bloom naturally, or could it sometimes be helped along?

* * *

Ever since yesterday's conversation with Maddie, Jake had been chewing on the notion of seeing a professional about his nightmares and flashbacks. He wasn't wild about the idea of giving somebody permission to poke around inside his mind, but the peace he'd felt yesterday after talking to Maddie had made him wonder if seeing a psychiatrist might do him some good.

He had no plans for the evening, so at his usual quitting time he left the office and climbed into his Beemer, intending to hit the highway and get some wind in his hair while he untangled his thoughts. Somehow he ended up on David Crockett Street, instead, and a minute later he found himself at the little park on the Prairie Springs River.

It was a good place to think. As the sun hung low over Fort Bonnell, Jake sat on a bench facing the placid river, arms folded and propped on his knees as he stared at the water's dark, glassy surface.

His thoughts darted in every direction, but mostly he wondered how to go about choosing a psychiatrist. What did other people do? Just ask their crazy friends for recommendations?

Another thing he wondered about was how to deal with the fact that he had once been a Christian but now wasn't sure what he believed. He didn't think he'd be comfortable spilling his guts to an atheist, but he didn't want some do-gooder Christian shoving God at him, either.

His thoughts were interrupted by the crunch of gravel under car tires in the parking lot behind him. Irritated that someone was about to interfere with his solitude, he glanced over his shoulder just in time to see Maddie's SUV roll to a stop beside his Beemer.

He sighed and sat up. Right on cue, his foolish heart had slipped into a double-time march. It was ridiculous, the way that woman controlled his pulse and respiration.

At least he wasn't in love with her, he consoled himself as he stared glumly at the river. He was certain of that. He was still wildly attracted to her, but those feelings could be managed. Time and discipline, that was all he needed. Time and—

"Honestly, Jake, I am *not* following you."

He turned. She had halted a few yards away and rested one hand on a tree trunk.

"This is my thinking spot." She lifted her chin, bravely defiant yet still achingly vulnerable. "I come here all the time."

"I didn't say anything, Madeline."

"I just don't want you thinking that I—"

"I'm not thinking anything at all." Good thing she wasn't a mind reader, because she'd have known there wasn't a speck of truth in that statement. Jake's mind was actually quite busy; he was thinking about how pretty her eyes were, and how much he wanted to push his fingers through the dark silk of her hair, and what it might feel like to kiss her bow-shaped mouth.

She walked over and sat down on the bench beside him. "Are you okay? You look…odd."

"I'm fine." Just coming a little unglued, but that was hardly a new development. He wondered if she knew any psychiatrists.

"Jake, as I said, this is my thinking spot." She spoke slowly, appearing to choose her words with the utmost care.

"And one of the things I came here just now to think about…is you."

"Why?" Frustration squeezed the word all the way up from his belly.

"Because I'm worried about you. I know you don't have any romantic interest in me, but didn't you feel relieved yesterday after our talk? That's what you need, Jake. Someone to talk to. A friend. And I happen to be available."

He considered telling her that he'd just about decided to see a psychiatrist, but that might prolong this conversation when he was desperate to shorten it and get away from Maddie before he said or did something he'd regret. "Madeline, I've never been any good at 'sharing.' That was one of Rita's biggest complaints, and I'm afraid I haven't changed in that respect."

Maddie sighed. "You know, it still upsets me to remember how she abandoned you."

Jake emitted a mirthless chuckle. "She was provoked, believe me."

"She left you in that hospital to rot. You had just lost your best friend and you barely made it yourself. She should have—"

"She had just started a new job in Austin," Jake interrupted. Rita had had her faults, but their marriage had crashed and burned because of his own selfishness, not because Rita had balked at getting on a plane. "She couldn't go running off to Germany. But she did visit me twice while I was at Walter Reed."

"She shouldn't have been 'visiting' you," Maddie huffed. "She should have been *with* you. Supporting you. Questioning your doctors. Bringing you cheeseburgers. Reminding you that you weren't alone. She was your *wife*."

"You don't understand." With the side of his right shoe, Jake dug at a little island of grass in the packed dirt in front of the bench. "She wanted me to leave the army, but I re-upped, and that last deployment put me on the fast track to destroying our marriage. All Rita ever wanted was for me to settle down with her in Texas."

"You couldn't have given up helicopters," Maddie said with quiet conviction. "You were just like Noah. You lived to fly."

With one last vicious kick, Jake freed the clump of grass from the dirt. "Maybe I should have lived for my wife."

"Maybe she should have tried harder to understand the man she married."

Jake snorted in bitter amusement. Twenty-six years old, and Maddie still had those stars in her eyes.

"I'm sure you made some mistakes," she continued. "But—"

"Too many to count, Madeline." Shame pricked him, but he couldn't allow her to believe he had ever been a good husband.

"But you're a different man now," she persisted. "You know where you went wrong, and you won't make those mistakes next time."

Jake wanted to hit something. Had there ever been a more pigheaded optimist than the woman beside him? Jake had presented evidence of his defective character and she had summarily dismissed it. He contained his frustration long enough to say, "There won't *be* a next time, Madeline."

"I'm praying that there will be, Jake." Her voice was as calm as the river's surface. "You deserve to be happy."

* * *

Maddie meant those words with all her heart. But while she had implied otherwise to Jake, she had begun to hope that *she* would be the woman to make him happy.

She suspected she'd been too quick to accuse Rita and defend Jake, but Jake appeared to be claiming more guilt than could have been rightfully his. Still, only God knew exactly what had happened in that marriage. All Maddie knew was that if Jake had wronged his wife, he was sorry for it, and if he married again, the woman he chose could safely trust him with her heart.

"You've always insisted on seeing me as a knight in shining armor." Jake stared at the river, his expression bleak. "But I'm just a man, Maddie." His turned to look at her. "And I'm not nearly as good a man as you think."

Yes, you are, her heart answered.

"Don't do that." His voice had deepened, and it rumbled like distant thunder as his eyelids dropped and his gaze fastened on her mouth. "Don't look at me that way."

"What way?" She was honestly unsure what he could be objecting to.

"I am not going to kiss you, Madeline." He negated the quiet authority of those words by leaning closer, his gaze still riveted to her mouth.

"That's fine, Jake." Encouraged by the sudden shift in his mood, she added, "But I'm definitely going to kiss *you*." Hardly able to believe her own boldness, she captured his face between her palms and pulled it down to her.

"No." Jake groaned the word, but a split second after their lips met, he surrendered with gratifying eagerness. His response was even more tender and thrilling than Maddie had dreamed it would be, but the kiss didn't last long. After Jake brought it to an end, he leaned away from her and stared, wide-eyed and worried, like a man who'd just been bitten by a rattlesnake.

"Jake?" she whispered uncertainly.

His eyes narrowed and a muscle in his jaw began to tic. "Don't you ever do that to me again," he said in a tight voice. He sprang up and snatched the cane he'd hooked over the back of the bench and stalked away.

Shattered, Maddie watched him go. What had she done that was so awful? She might have behaved a little recklessly, but once that kiss had gotten underway, Jake had been no unwilling participant.

In the gathering twilight, she stared blindly at the river and fought to understand what had just transpired. *Don't you ever do that to me again,* he'd said, as though by kissing him she had hurt him in some way. But how could that be?

Emerging slowly from the mists of her mind, the answer began to coalesce. With words and actions, Jake had told her repeatedly that he wasn't going to get involved with her. He had even told her why: because he feared he'd end up breaking her heart.

Jake must have seen that kiss as a betrayal of Noah's trust and of his own honor. So Maddie *had* hurt him.

"Lord, forgive me," she whispered as hot tears filled her eyes. "I was too wrapped up in what I was feeling to realize what I was tempting him to do."

And that, according to her mama, wasn't true love.

Appalled by what he had just done, Jake flung himself into his car. What had he been thinking, kissing Maddie? After all his insistence that there could never be anything between them, he had undermined his credibility by kissing her.

What must she be thinking right now? That he hadn't meant a word of what he'd said, obviously. That had been clear enough after the kiss, when she'd looked at him with star-filled eyes.

This *could not* happen. Noah would have flattened him for kissing Maddie like that, and he'd have been right to do it. Sweet Maddie deserved better than a tormented ex-pilot who didn't have a clue how to make a woman happy.

Jake turned his key in the ignition. His CD player powered up and George Strait put in his two cents' worth, sliding smoothly into the chorus of "Nobody in His Right Mind Would Have Left Her," a song about a foolish man who'd turned his back on the woman of his dreams. Jake jabbed at the button, silencing the player.

There were times in a man's life when even George Strait was no help at all.

Chapter Twelve

Operating on the assumption that busy women didn't have time to suffer from broken hearts, Maddie was determined to fill her free hours with more church and charitable activities than ever before. She hadn't slept well the previous night, not after that awful scene with Jake, but that had given her an idea. From now on, she meant to be so exhausted every time her head hit the pillow that she wouldn't have to search for sleep. It would come and find her.

In the middle of her shift at the hospital, Maddie was washing her hands in the women's room when she glanced in the mirror and noticed purple crescents under her eyes and frown lines enclosing her mouth like a set of parentheses. As she reached for a paper towel, a hank of hair slipped out of the clip at the back of her head and fell against her cheek.

Inside and out, she was a mess. Sighing, she unhitched the clip and finger-combed her hair.

"There you are." Myrna Alsop, the civilian nurse who had been tasked with teaching and mentoring Maddie, stood just inside the doorway. With her trim shape and perfect posture, her tidy black hair and alert green eyes, Myrna was always the picture of efficiency.

Maddie refastened her hair clip and looked inquiringly at her preceptor.

"I'm concerned about you," Myrna said.

Maddie braced herself. "Have I done something wrong?"

"No. I merely want to remind you that you can't give less of yourself to your patients just because you're having problems in your personal life."

Maddie opened her mouth to ask where she had fallen short, but Myrna shook her head.

"It wasn't an accusation. Just a warning. You're an excellent nurse, and I'd hate to see you lower your standards."

"Yes, ma'am," Maddie said quietly. Myrna's mentoring style was more demanding than encouraging, but she was never unfair.

"Is there anything you want to talk about?" Myrna asked.

"No, ma'am. I just didn't get a good night's sleep. It won't happen again."

On her break Maddie went to look in on Ali, who wasn't yet well enough to return home. As she started down the corridor toward his room, she noticed a tall, dark-haired man leaning against the wall reading a newspaper.

"Excuse me," he said when Maddie reached him. "Have you seen Dr. Nora Blake?"

"Not today," Maddie said courteously. "But if you'll go to the desk, they can tell you if she's in the hospital."

Folding his newspaper, he nodded toward Ali's room. "Are you going in there?"

Maddie stiffened. "Why do you ask?"

He smiled. "Sorry. I'm Robert Dale, reporter for *Liberty*

and Justice. I'd like to ask Dr. Blake a couple of questions about Ali Willis."

So he could write a sensational story about the boy's troubles? Maddie eyed the man coldly. "Mr. Dale, I doubt that she'll be eager to speak to you. I don't know Dr. Blake well, but I understand she has strong feelings about people who exploit the sufferings of children to sell newspapers."

His polite smile, which had begun to fade as Maddie spoke, suddenly widened into a grin. "So I've been given to understand. But that's not what I'm after. I just want—"

"Here she comes now," Maddie interrupted, looking past him. She couldn't wait to see the blond beauty her fellow nurses called "Dr. Ice Princess" freeze out this obnoxious reporter.

Robert Dale turned. Dr. Blake spotted him and did an about-face, striding back in the direction from which she'd come. Robert Dale loped after her, calling her name. She opened a door marked Hospital Staff Only and stepped through to the restricted area. She turned and watched the reporter with a stony expression, then deliberately closed the door just as he reached it.

He stared at the closed door for a moment, then looked at Maddie and spread his arms and shrugged. As she chuckled at the comical, self-deprecating gesture, he touched the folded newspaper to his forehead in a casual salute and went on his way.

Maddie stared after him, wondering, then she gave herself a little shake, fixed a smile on her face and strolled into Ali's room. Just inside the doorway, she halted and clasped her hands over her heart.

With his booted feet on the white-blanketed hospital bed,

retired general Marlon Willis lay on his back with Ali cradled in the crook of his arm. The boy hugged Texas Bear and gazed raptly at his grandfather, who was reading aloud from what appeared to be a book of Bible stories.

Maddie was utterly charmed. How could she ever have thought the general lacked a tender side? Glad that her soft-soled shoes hadn't announced her presence, she backed out of the room and said a silent prayer for Ali and his grandfather.

Returning to her own floor, she had just reached the nurses' station when she heard an anxious male voice behind her.

"Lieutenant Bright? Ma'am, if I could just have a word?"

Used to reassuring nervous fathers-to be, Maddie turned and smiled at the tall private whose fatigues hung on his skinny frame as if they'd been draped over a broomstick. "How can I help you?"

He rubbed a hand over his buzz-cut blond hair. "Ma'am, I know there's no way you'll remember me, but four months ago, you helped patch me up after I caught some shrapnel from an IED."

Maddie didn't remember him, and she felt terrible about that. But there had been so many of them, and injuries from improvised explosive devices were, tragically, something she'd seen nearly every day.

"I was worried about what would happen to my parents and my little sister if I died," the soldier continued earnestly. "You took the time to listen to me, ma'am. You even…" He stopped and looked nervously around him, then lowered his voice. "Ma'am, you even prayed for me once."

It would have been more than once, although he wouldn't know that. She'd prayed for all of them, constantly. She glanced at the name patch on his uniform. "I'm glad my prayers were answered, Private Gaffney. You're looking well."

"Thank you, ma'am. And thank you for what you did for me."

What *she* did for *him?* "Nursing soldiers like you was a privilege," she said with a little quaver in her voice. Every day had been a struggle, but the past year had been the most meaningful of her life. Why was she just now realizing that?

"Thank you for what *you* did over there," she added. His service had been much greater than hers. Private Gaffney had put his life on the line for the sake of their country.

His thin face broke into a smile and he looked even younger. "That's all I wanted, ma'am. Just to say thanks." His smile disappeared as he snapped to attention and saluted.

Hiding her surprise, Maddie acknowledged the salute. Private Gaffney held his for a full five seconds after she lowered her arm. Dazed, she watched him turn smartly and walk away.

"I'm still fuzzy on army protocol," Myrna said as she came to stand beside Maddie. "But I didn't think you people bothered with saluting indoors." Her gaze skimmed meaningfully over Maddie's scrubs. "Or when you're not in uniform."

"He wasn't required to salute." Overwhelmed by the emotions crashing through her, Maddie struggled to make her voice audible. "He did it to honor me."

"That's what I thought. And I have to tell you, it choked me up."

"They were so brave," Maddie whispered. Mere words could never describe the heroism she had repeatedly witnessed while nursing men like Private Gaffney, but words were all she had. "Even when they were critically injured, I couldn't so much as fluff a pillow without hearing a feeble, 'Thank you, ma'am.' They never forgot their training, even when they were in terrible pain. They never forgot their mission or their buddies, either. They all wanted to know how soon they'd be able to rejoin their units."

Unashamed, she wiped away a tear. "You just can't imagine how fine and noble they were. Every one of them. Until you've been privileged to see that, there's just no way you can truly understand."

She felt her mouth tremble as she smiled. "I've never told anybody that."

"I suspected you had a tough time of it over there," Myrna said thoughtfully.

"It was the hardest year of my life," Maddie admitted. "I pray that God never asks me to go back there. But for the first time, I'm...*grateful*. Does that make any sense?"

"Yes, it does. But, Maddie, I hope you don't think the nursing you're doing now is less important than what you were doing overseas. If you think that, you're cheating your patients."

Maddie nodded, remembering what Jake had said about all nurses being heroes. "I'm beginning to understand that." A little sheepishly, she added, "I think God's giving me an attitude overhaul."

Myrna smiled before resuming her usual brisk demeanor. "Ready to get back to work?"

"Yes, ma'am." Maddie was more ready than she had ever been.

On Friday afternoon Gloria walked into Jake's office, ostensibly to water plants. Jake was busy answering e-mails from clients, but didn't miss the furtive glances Gloria kept shooting his way as she puttered around the room. When she walked over to the window and tipped the spout of her watering can into something green and leafy, Jake exchanged a look with Tripod and shrugged.

"Your friend Olga Terenkov is chasing our preacher," Gloria said.

"Hmm." Jake hoped his bored tone would nip that discussion in the bud. Gloria was a good-hearted woman, but she had a lamentable inclination to stick her nose into other people's business.

"He's been widowed for years and it's time he got married again. They're perfect for each other, if you ask me."

"I didn't," Jake pointed out in the same flat voice as he typed a few more words.

"She's not being real subtle about it," Gloria said. "But some men can be dense, if you know what I mean."

Jake's fingers stilled on his keyboard. Something about this one-sided conversation was beginning to worry him.

"I had to chase Leland until he caught me," Gloria continued. "Back in his prime that man rode some of the meanest bulls in Texas. But do you think he had enough courage to ask me to dance?" She barked out a laugh. "No, sir. He did not."

"Is there a point to this?" Jake asked, desperately hoping there wasn't. Because if there was, she was undoubtedly planning to stab him with it.

"I'm just saying there's something about being in love that tends to scare the boots off a man."

Travis, who had strolled into Jake's office in the middle of that sentence, turned on his heel and scurried back through the doorway faster than a retreating cockroach. From the safety of the hall, he snickered.

"Hey, thanks for the support," Jake called after him.

Undaunted by the interruption, Gloria set her watering can on the floor, folded her plump arms over her chest and continued, the gleam in her eyes half amused, half scornful. "I honestly don't know why so many women complain about men being hard to understand. Y'all are as simple as peach pie. See, a man wants to feel he's in control of his life. So when some pretty girl comes along and steals his heart, he's terrified. He doesn't want to be vulnerable to anyone, especially a woman who can twist him round her little finger. So he'll tie himself in knots trying to convince himself he's not in love. And—" Jake's intercom buzzed.

Profoundly grateful for the interruption, Jake leaned forward and pressed the button.

"Ms. Lopez is here for your three-thirty," Lexi said.

"Send her in," Jake replied, watching Gloria from under raised eyebrows. *"Quick."*

Gloria's bottom lip poked out; she was clearly disappointed that she wasn't going to be able to finish her lecture. But she'd lost Jake right after that part about peach pie, anyway.

"We'll talk later." She bent to pick up her watering can.

"I'll be busy later," Jake said. "But if you still feel the need to talk to somebody, I'm sure Travis will be free."

She gave him an amused snort in response to that and bustled out of his office.

Jake shook his head at the empty doorway and wondered where on earth she'd picked up the crazy idea that he was in love.

* * *

Jake had season's tickets to the Longhorns' games, but he'd given Saturday's pair to Travis so he could spend that afternoon and evening with his mama. She'd been putting on a brave face, but she still missed Jake's father terribly, and Jake was convinced that the recent scare over the lump in her breast had affected her more than she was letting on.

He took her out to lunch, then devoted the remainder of the day to fixing leaky sinks and performing other chores around the ranch-style house he'd grown up in. It was late when he finished, so he opted to spend the night instead of driving home.

Awakened the next morning by a blast of country music, Jake opened his eyes and stared at the light fixture on the ceiling of his old room and wondered what his mama was doing playing a George Strait CD at—he turned his head to look at the beside clock—seven in the morning.

It wasn't that Jake minded being awakened. He didn't have any objection to mornings, except for the moment when he had to put weight on his left leg after being off it for hours. And he was glad to know she still had good taste in music. But as he shuffled to the shower, goose bumps prickled his shoulders and he sensed something unusual in the air, something almost like the drop in pressure that heralded the arrival of a summer storm.

He had the strongest feeling that while he'd slept, the world had begun to change in some material way.

In jeans and bare feet and a gray University of Texas T-shirt, his wet hair slicked back, Jake padded down the hall to the kitchen. On any other morning the aromas of yeasty cinnamon rolls and frying bacon would have made his belly rumble with anticipation, but right now he was worried. It was out of character for his mother to play music before breakfast, especially at this decibel level. Jake's jaw nearly hit the floor when he reached the kitchen and saw what was going on in there.

Dancing.

In a flowery blue dress covered in front by a ruffled white apron, with her mostly gray hair already curled and sprayed for church, his mama was Texas two-stepping and twirling her way around the kitchen table. She looked pretty, Jake thought, but she'd gone crazy on him.

"*Mama?*"

She looked at him and grinned, but kept dancing, her arms gracefully extended as though embracing an invisible partner. It was no mystery who she imagined holding her, because to Jake's knowledge she had never danced with any man but his father.

Jake glanced at the stove, where bacon sizzled in an iron skillet, and wondered if it was safe for a woman in her condition to be cooking. Would he have to put her in one of those homes for seniors who weren't quite themselves anymore?

"Dance with me," she invited.

Jake gaped at her. Had she forgotten? "Mama, my dancing days were over years ago."

She lifted her arms over her head and twirled away from him. "Take the bacon off the fire and dance with me."

"Mama, I can't dance," he said patiently.

"If a man can walk, he can dance."

It was on the tip of Jake's tongue to point out that he wasn't that great a walker, but his father had taught him never to contradict his mama. "Yes, ma'am," he said obediently, wondering how on earth he was going to manage dancing. He switched off the electric burner under the bacon, then grabbed a Texas-shaped potholder and slid the skillet off the hot coils. When he turned around, his mother held out her arms to him.

Bracing himself with his cane, he rested his left hand against her back and wondered how to proceed. Slow dancing, he might have managed. But the energetic two-step called for him to scoot her around the floor and do a good bit of twirling.

He took a few experimental steps. He was as awkward as his three-legged cat, but his mama didn't seem to care. Her face was radiant, he noticed as he caught her hand and raised it over her head.

"What's up with you?" he asked.

She flashed a brilliant smile as she twirled under his arm. "I'm celebrating life!"

"Well, that's good." Jake smiled back, but he was still vaguely worried.

His mama patted his shoulder. "I thought I wanted to die after your daddy did, but in my talk with God this morning I was thanking Him again for the biopsy results when I realized just how badly I want to live. Life is *good*, Jake, and I've been letting it pass me by. I've decided to start enjoying it again."

That little speech had pushed a lump into Jake's throat, so he just nodded and raised her hand again.

She turned gracefully. "I've missed dancing."

As George Strait sang "I Just Want to Dance with You," Jake wondered what it would be like to hold Maddie in his arms and twirl her around the floor. He'd never know, but that was for the best. He just hoped that one day she'd find a man who...

No.

Jake's steps halted and a loud buzzing commenced in his brain as everything in him rebelled against the idea of Maddie spending her life with another man. There was no way in the world that such a thing could ever be right. Not when she loved him and he...

"I made your favorite cinnamon rolls." His mama went to turn off the oven timer, the source of the buzz Jake had mistaken for a warning that his brain was redlining. "And I'm fixin' to scramble you some eggs," she added as she switched off the CD player and put the bacon on to finish cooking.

Behind his mother's back, Jake's mouth worked, shaping Maddie's name without sound.

Surely if a man wanted to do it badly enough, he could learn how to make a woman happy. He could be a different man. A *better* man. He could make things right with God and he could...

Jake slumped onto a chair, dazed by the thoughts that were tearing through his mind. Even before that last deployment, he'd begun to wander away from God. More and more, he had gone his own selfish way, so when the crisis came he'd been wholly unprepared to weather it. Crushed by grief, drowning in guilt, he had given himself over to bitterness instead of seeking God's forgiveness and help.

He had ended up with a heart so badly bruised that he'd tried to shut it down so he couldn't be hurt anymore.

He had wasted more than five years of his life. Just plain *wasted* them, because God had been right here all along. And like the prodigal son, Jake could have come home at any time.

It wasn't too late, he realized as his mother set a mug of

coffee in front of him. He'd told Maddie he wasn't sure he believed, but that had been a lie. All these years, he'd been living a lie.

"I *do* believe," he said aloud. Why had he fought so hard to deny the truths he'd known since boyhood?

"What's that?" his mother asked as she turned the bacon slices with a fork.

Jake hadn't realized he'd given voice to his thoughts. He opened his mouth to say it was nothing, but then he decided if he was going to make a new start, he was going to do the thing right. "Forget the bacon, Mama, and sit down a minute." When she turned to look at him, concern widening her brown eyes and deepening every line in her sweet face, he held out both hands to her.

As she took them and settled onto a chair, Jake drew a long breath and then asked a question she'd probably been waiting years to hear. "Will you pray with me, Mama?"

Chapter Thirteen

From her front door, Alma Jean Hopkins waved goodbye to her only child and watched him back his convertible out of her driveway. Uncharacteristically distracted, Jake had forgotten to kiss her goodbye. Even more surprising, he had walked away from his favorite breakfast.

Alma Jean couldn't have been more delighted, although she had closed her eyes just now and said a brief prayer that he'd pay sufficient attention to his driving.

God had done some marvelous things this morning, she reflected as she fingered the thin rope of pearls at her neck, pearls her beloved Connor had given her the morning after she'd presented him with their son. She had decades' worth of good memories she could sift through whenever she wanted, but this morning her future looked mighty promising.

More importantly, so did Jake's.

Humming a favorite hymn, she shut the front door and returned to her kitchen.

She didn't have to look up Marva Bright's phone number because she'd put it on speed dial a few weeks ago. She picked up the phone and pressed one key, then fidgeted impatiently while Marva's phone rang. If she didn't unload some of this joy on somebody right now, her poor heart was going to burst.

"Marva?" In her eagerness, she interrupted her friend's hello. "Marva, I have wonderful news. Jake stayed the night with me, and this morning at breakfast he asked me to pray with him. He finally settled everything with God, and right now he's scootin' back to Prairie Springs to see that girl of yours."

"Praise the Lord!" Marva crowed. "We've waited a long time to see that boy get back on the right path. I don't mind telling you, Alma Jean, I was fit to be tied the other night when I realized Maddie was in love with him. You know I always thought of him as one of my own, but I didn't want him romancin' Maddie before he made things right with the Lord."

Alma Jean understood. She had begun to wonder if they'd been wrong to pray about their kids falling in love. Maybe they shouldn't have done that until after God had answered their *first* prayer, the one about Jake reconciling with the Lord. But Maddie was wrapped up in her nursing career and had never been serious about a man, while Jake had a pile of problems to work out before he could be good for *any* woman, never mind Maddie, so their mamas had assumed it would take a lot of praying and a lot of waiting before the desired results were achieved.

How could they have guessed that Maddie would ask her mama for advice about love before she had even had an actual date with Jake? And how could they have guessed that Jake would decide—again, without going on a single date— to hightail it back to Prairie Springs and propose to the girl?

"I never dreamed they'd fall in love so fast," Marva said.

"I hear you."

"But listen, hon, I was just on my way out the door to church. Why don't I call you later?"

Alma Jean looked at the clock on her stove. "I'd better hustle, too. Our service starts at nine. I just couldn't wait to tell you the good news. Boy howdy, do we have a lot to celebrate this morning!"

"We sure do." Maddie's mother paused. "Should we tell the kids we prayed them together?"

Alma Jean pondered that. "No," she said slowly. "You remember how it was, don't you, Marva? When you and your man were the only two people in the world? If we told the kids we had something to do with this, they wouldn't believe us. So let's just save this story for our grandchildren."

Maddie's mother emitted a bubbly laugh. "Great minds think alike, Alma Jean."

Chapter Fourteen

Sliding his sunglasses on, Jake gloried in the warmth of the morning sun on his face and the cool wind ripping through his hair as his Beemer roared down the highway. As George Strait's rich voice boomed out "This is the Big One," a song about a man who's just realized he's in love, Jake laughed out loud and punched up the volume.

He couldn't wait to tell Maddie he had actually danced this morning. He couldn't wait to give *her* a twirl. Tapping his fingers on the steering wheel in time with the song, he accompanied George in an enthusiastic if slightly rusty baritone.

He had never dreamed he could feel this exhilarated when he wasn't sitting in a helicopter. He'd believed he had already tasted the best life had to offer. He'd thought nothing could ever be that good again.

He had been wrong.

The road stretching before him on this sunny Sunday morning suggested he might go anywhere, do anything. With Maddie at his side and God leading them both…

Maddie.

Wonder of wonders, Gloria had nailed it. He *had* been afraid of giving up control. But now he'd gone and done it: he'd fallen in love.

Travis was going to bust a gut laughing. No doubt he'd make some crack about Jake having "outgrown" his allergy. Gloria would probably cry, just like Jake's mama had. And Maddie? Well, he was hoping Madeline Bright would do him the very great honor of becoming his wife.

He already knew she was in love with him. Even if she hadn't all but said so at the barbecue, she'd told him with those gorgeous eyes of hers at least a hundred times, and he wasn't going to let her take it back.

He wanted to walk beside her for the rest of his days. As far as it was in his power, he meant to sweeten her life. If Whitney and John came home, if Ali's surgery went well, he wanted to share Maddie's joy. And if her heart got broken, he'd share *that*. He'd hold her while she cried, and then he'd pray with her and help her get through the dark days of her grief.

As he neared Prairie Springs, Jake glanced at his watch. He didn't know what time church started, but he could swing by there on the way home and check the sign out front. Then he'd go put on his best suit with the blue tie Maddie had said she liked. Dapper, she'd called him that day at the general's house.

He'd show that woman dapper. He glanced in his rearview mirror and pulled out to pass a slow-moving eighteen-wheeler. "Out of my way, bubba," he hollered like the lovesick fool he was. "I'm in a hurry to do some courtin'."

But he was going to church first. If Maddie wasn't there, he'd go to the hospital after the service and find her. He'd sit patiently in the waiting room until she got off or could at least take a meal break, and then he'd propose.

He didn't plan to rush her. If she needed time, she could have it. But Jake didn't intend to waste a single minute of the new life God had given him. Now that he knew what he wanted, he was going after her.

His mama had laughed when he'd said that. But then she'd given Jake her blessing and her one-and-a-half-carat diamond engagement ring. He'd had neither when he'd impulsively married Rita in Las Vegas all those years ago.

Jake had thanked her and then asked, "Mama, what was Dad's secret? What did he do that made you so happy?"

Her eyes had grown misty, and she'd told him that Connor Hopkins had always put her needs before his own, even when he hadn't felt like it. His unswerving dedication to that ideal had encouraged her to do the same for him. "And that," she had concluded, "is the secret of a happy marriage."

That made sense to Jake. With God's help, he would never hurt Maddie the way he had hurt Rita.

Back at the house, Jake had offered all of himself to God. He had asked to be allowed to have Maddie for his wife, but even if the Lord had other plans for her, Jake would never regret the decision he'd made this morning. Because even before his heart was Maddie's, it was God's.

From now on, he was God's man, eager to serve at His command.

Chapter Fifteen

"And at five minutes before ten o'clock on this last day of September, it's a comfortable seventy-two degrees here in downtown Austin," the radio announcer's voice boomed over the end of an old Trisha Yearwood song. Maddie stopped at a red light and signaled for a turn into the parking lot of Prairie Springs Christian Church. It was a gorgeous blue-sky morning, and she was trying to appreciate that, but after working all night and helping to deliver two babies, she was bone-tired. Immediately after church, she would go home and crawl into bed.

Home. Soon that word would mean a little blue house on Pecan Street. She'd signed the lease/purchase agreement just yesterday, and would be able to move in two weeks.

The first thing she planned to do after moving her things was plant some pink roses for Whitney. Whether they would turn out to be a memorial or simply an investment for Whitney's future enjoyment, only God knew. Maddie had admitted to herself that Whitney and John might never come home, but it wasn't wrong to hope and pray otherwise, so she meant to keep doing that. Just yesterday, she'd said as much to Olga as they'd stuffed some care packages Children of the Day was sending overseas to war victims.

Olga was easy to talk to, so Maddie had poured out her heart to the older woman. It felt good to talk after keeping her troubles to herself for so long. And Olga had gently suggested that Maddie could encourage others without pretending she didn't have worries of her own. Prompted by Jake's comments on that subject, Maddie had already been praying about that and had reached the same conclusion.

Life would never be easy and it would never be without heartache, but Maddie was determined that from now on, it would be good. She had given herself fully to God and was trusting Him with her future.

That didn't mean she hadn't been crying over Jake. But she believed God would heal that hurt in time. She'd thought about going to Jake and apologizing for the way she'd thrown herself at him, but she figured he'd rather be left alone. Maybe one day the two of them could be real friends. But for now, she meant to stay out of his way—not an easy thing to do in a town the size of Prairie Springs.

The light changed and Maddie made her left turn. She snagged one of the last available spaces in the church lot and had just climbed out of her SUV when she spotted Jake not thirty feet away.

What was he doing here, wearing a suit and looking like he meant to go to church with everyone else? Maddie had prayed and prayed that he would turn back to the Lord, and if he was going to church, she would rejoice about that. But she didn't want to get in the way of his reconciliation with God, and she *did* have an amazing gift for arousing his temper.

Nervously smoothing wrinkles from the skirt of her yellow floral silk dress, she considered her options. She didn't think he'd seen her; someone had just called a greeting to him, and he'd turned his head and said something back. For the space of three seconds, Maddie thought about diving behind a car until he'd passed. But hiding from Jake was a childish idea.

She decided to run.

Or at least, walk very, very quickly. It was Sunday morning and this was the church parking lot, she admonished herself as she hastened to the church steps. A certain amount of decorum was called for.

"Maddie!"

She stumbled. Had he actually called her name? She looked nervously over her shoulder and saw him moving faster than she would have thought possible, his endearingly awkward gait aided by a black cane that gleamed in the sunlight. She offered him a tremulous smile and a shaky little wave, then turned back toward the church, walking even faster.

"Maddie, wait!"

This time when she turned around, she was stunned to see him actually running the last few steps toward her, although *lurching* was probably a more apt description. Instinctively she stretched out her arms to catch him, but his momentum knocked them both off balance.

Somehow he managed to twist his body so that he hit the pavement first. As she came down on top of his legs, he grunted in pain.

Appalled, she tried to scramble off him, but his arms tightened around her and he held her on his right knee.

"Caught you!" he said, grinning crookedly.

But why had he chased her? And why did he look so happy? Didn't his leg hurt? "Let me go," Maddie yelped, completely unnerved.

Beaming at her, he gave his head a little shake. "I *tried* to let you go. I'm sorry, but that wasn't working for me." His smile faded suddenly and his brown eyes widened in earnest entreaty. "This morning I asked God to forgive me, and now I'm asking you to do the same. I know I don't deserve it, Maddie, but I'm hoping you love me enough to make some allowances for an idiot who loves you more than he'll ever be able to put into words."

He pressed his mouth againfst hers and for a moment, she was too startled to respond.

But only for a moment. This was *Jake,* and she wanted to kiss him more than she wanted to breathe.

She actually heard bells. Somebody laughed. And she heard Gloria Ridge say in tones of deep amusement, "Hallelujah, the boy's finally figured it out!"

Embarrassed, Maddie opened her eyes and pushed away from Jake. He immediately grasped her head and tried to pull her back, but Maddie resisted. "We have an audience!" she said in an urgent whisper.

Gloria tapped Jake on the shoulder with his ebony walking stick. "Come on now, kids," she drawled. "You're blocking traffic."

When Jake took the cane, Gloria reached for Maddie's hands and pulled her to her feet. Leland helped Jake get up.

An unknown old lady harrumphed as she walked by. "Fine behavior in the church parking lot!"

Maddie would have been mortified if she hadn't been so

deliciously besotted with the handsome brown-eyed man who was gazing at her as though she was the only woman in the world.

"If you ask me," Gloria said loudly, "the church parking lot is an excellent place for a marriage proposal."

Maddie groaned softly. *Now* she was mortified.

Jake just grinned and lifted one dark eyebrow at her.

"Come on, Gloria," Leland said to his wife. "The boy don't need any help with his courtin'." He draped an arm around her and led her away.

The handful of people they'd been unwittingly entertaining drifted away, too. Only then did Maddie realize that the bells she'd heard while kissing Jake had been the chimes calling the worshippers to the service.

"Church is starting," she said, avoiding his rapt gaze by brushing some imaginary dust off the sleeve of his suit coat. "Are you coming in?"

"Yes, in a minute. First I thought I'd take Gloria's suggestion and propose to you."

He couldn't possibly mean that. Nobody got engaged after just two kisses. Unable to meet his eyes, Maddie reached for his tie to straighten it while she tried to think of a suitable response to his teasing.

He trapped her hands under one of his and pressed them hard against his chest. Surprised by the rapid pounding of his heart, she looked up and encountered his unbelievably tender gaze.

"Are you really proposing to me?" she asked in a breathy whisper.

"Not at the moment. Right now I'm trying to determine whether it's physically possible for me to go down on one knee. I could probably do it, but I'd need you to help me up again, and I'm thinking that could be a real mood killer."

"Oh, Jake!" She pressed her fingers over her mouth and started to cry. After a few seconds she composed herself enough to say, rather primly, she thought, "I'll be happy to accept a standing-up proposal."

"All right. Here it comes." Jake cleared his throat. "Madeline Bright, will you—"

"Yes!" She threw her arms around his neck. If this wasn't real, if it was just some kind of wonderful dream, she prayed she would never, ever wake up.

"You didn't let me finish." He gently peeled her off his chest. "As I was saying, will you please go to church with me—"

"What?" Laughing through her tears, she smacked his shoulder. "What happened to my proposal?"

His dark eyes danced with mischief. "Maybe if you'd stop interrupting, I could get to that." He pressed the tip of her nose with his index finger. "Madeline Bright, will you please go to church with me…as my future wife?"

She lost her grin. "I will. I love you, Jake." She sniffled and then ran a fingertip under each of her eyes, catching tears and no doubt smearing mascara everywhere. "I can't believe you love me back," she squeaked out.

"It'll be my pleasure to convince you." He crushed her against him and kissed her again, then he whispered in her ear, "I love the way you smell."

She never wore any kind of perfume, so he had to be talking about her hair. "It's just baby shampoo," she said almost apologetically.

He chuckled. "I know." He kissed the side of her head,

then shifted his weight and reached into his pocket. "Will you wear my mama's engagement ring?"

"Oh!" She nodded hard. "Yes." She hadn't realized until this moment just how sentimental she was, but the idea of wearing his family heirloom made her cry again. When Jake took her hand and pushed a big platinum-mounted marquise diamond onto her finger, she saw little more than a sparkly blur.

Jake lifted her hand and kissed the ring on her finger. Then he kissed her mouth, which turned out to be a little awkward because they were both smiling so hard.

Lost in a pair of eyes the color of bluebonnets, Jake didn't notice the throbbing of the approaching rotors until Maddie tipped her head and looked skyward. For an instant Jake felt the familiar dread, but Maddie's presence anchored him.

"I have flashbacks," he blurted.

Her gaze dropped to his face. "I know."

"And nightmares." She would have to know all of it sooner or later.

"I wondered," she said, perfectly composed.

He should have told her these things before asking her to marry him, but they had honestly slipped his mind. He thought she would understand, though, because she was a nurse and because she was Maddie. He told her the rest. "I…need to see somebody."

"I've heard good things about Dr. Raleigh," she said as calmly as if she was suggesting a restaurant for dinner. Pitching her voice to be heard above the whine of the approaching engines and the staccato whirling of rotors, she added, "I'll get his phone number for you."

The helicopters screamed directly overhead. Jake kept his eyes on Maddie, trusting her love to hold him.

"Look up," she urged. "Look up and say a prayer for those brave men."

He wasn't sure what would happen, but he had Maddie to cling to. So for the first time in five years, Jake lifted his head to gaze at a pair of Apaches ripping through the bright blue sky.

It hurt, but not the way he'd feared it would. This was a whole new kind of pain; he was stabbed so hard by pride and gratitude that for a moment he couldn't catch his breath.

"You should always look up." Maddie snuggled against his side as he watched the helicopters grow smaller in the sapphire sky. "Who knows better than you what challenges those men will face in the coming months and years? Pray for them, Jake."

Unable to speak, he replied with a jerky nod and then sent a silent, heartfelt petition to God for the preservation and protection of the four crew members of the Apaches that were now mere specks next to a blinding-white cloud.

As Maddie had suggested, Jake knew exactly how to pray for the pilots. He knew the things they worried about but never talked about. He knew all the bad things that could happen to their helicopters—and to *them*. He knew that while they were insanely in love with flying, they were also dead serious about their duty to their country. And he knew that although they had everything to live for, they were prepared to die for the cause of freedom.

He was proud of them all.

"Jake?" Maddie nudged him.

He looked down at her. "I loved flying with Noah." His

voice came out gravelly, so he cleared his throat. "But even when we weren't flying, it was a privilege to be his friend."

Maddie leaned her face against his shoulder. "He felt the same way about you."

Jake pulled her back into his arms and squeezed hard. "We'll talk about him, Maddie. As much as you want."

She made a soft sound of grief against the lapel of his suit, and Jake just held on tight. They stood that way for a minute and then he said, "I'll have to tell your mother what really happened."

Maddie stiffened in his arms. "Mama *knows* what happened. Noah was killed while you were trying to save him. The only thing you need to explain to Mama is why you haven't seen her in all this time."

Jake winced.

"You weren't responsible for Noah's death," Maddie insisted quietly.

He sighed. "I'm trying to believe that. I don't feel the guilt I did before, but I still wonder how things would have turned out if I had made a different decision that night."

She relaxed against him. "Jake, all of life is that way. We make the best decisions we can, and then we leave the results in God's hands. Things don't always go the way we think they should. But do you remember what Job said to his wife? 'Shall we accept good from God, and not trouble?'" Maddie leaned back and searched Jake's face with her amazing blue eyes. "I don't know why the Lord took Noah. But understand this, Jake—it *was* the Lord who took him. You didn't have anything to do with it."

"I'll give that some thought," he promised, relaxing his hold on her. "But right now, I want to go to church."

"Me, too."

"Wait." He smoothed down a renegade wisp of her dark hair. Then with the pad of his thumb, he rubbed a dark smudge of makeup from under her left eye.

She stood still for his ministrations, then picked a strand of her hair off his shirt collar and straightened his tie. "Okay, we're ready." She took his hand.

The sermon had already begun, so they slipped quietly into one of the back pews. As Jake sat beside Maddie, an indescribable peace settled over his heart.

Pastor Franklin Fields spoke to the small but rapt congregation about sacrificial love. When he mentioned the apostle Paul's exhortation in Ephesians 5:25 that husbands should love their wives as Christ loved the church, the words "…and gave himself for it" rang like bells in Jake's mind.

So that was it. His father's secret for keeping his wife happy had come straight from the Bible.

Jake couldn't wait to be alone with Maddie, but after the service, his little ray of sunshine insisted on greeting and hugging everyone she saw. Jake noticed a few familiar faces, but even the strangers were quick to welcome him to their church and offer congratulations on his engagement.

Maddie introduced him to Pastor Fields. They talked for a minute, and when the pastor excused himself to speak to someone else, Maddie turned to Jake, sighed happily and said, "I guess we can go now."

Finally.

As they reached the church entrance, Olga Terenkov rushed past without seeing them. Maddie turned and would have called to her, but Olga had already stopped to speak to another friend.

"We'll see her later," Jake said, applying gentle pressure to the small of Maddie's back to get her moving again. As he turned, he noticed the pastor frowning at Olga's profile and did a double take, remembering what Gloria had said about the pair.

Jake knew a kindred spirit when he saw one. Amused, he put his mouth next to Maddie's ear and murmured, "I think your pastor's bachelor days are numbered."

"What?"

"The man's falling in love, Maddie."

She looked at the pastor and followed his tortured gaze to Olga, who gestured animatedly as she talked to her friend. "Why do you say that? He just looks…" Her forehead furrowed as she sought the right word.

"Perplexed?" Jake suggested. "Poleaxed? Confounded? Mystified? Scared mindless? I'm telling you, Maddie, he's about to fall and fall hard."

Laughing, she shook her head. "I will never understand men."

"I don't know why not," Jake said, belatedly marveling at his office manager's perspicacity. "We're as simple as peach pie."

He looked back at the pastor. *Give in,* he wanted to tell the man. *Love isn't anything to be afraid of because love never destroys.*

Love is what heals us all.

Chapter Sixteen

Half an hour later Maddie rested her chin on her hand and sighed as she watched her fiancé scoop salsa onto a tortilla chip.

"Why did you want to come here?" Jake asked. "You're so tired you can't even eat your lunch."

That was true. She'd taken just two bites of her chicken enchilada. "I don't want to leave you," she said baldly.

Fighting a grin, Jake aimed a forkful of guacamole at her mouth. She opened obediently.

She'd suggested lunch at this Mexican restaurant because it was one of the few places in Prairie Springs that was open at noon on Sunday but not filled to the rafters with the brunch crowd. Maddie hadn't wanted to take a chance on being approached by friends who would be eager to chat, so she'd brought Jake to this dim, quiet restaurant where she could sit next to him in a high-backed corner booth and sneak kisses.

She just hoped she could stay awake for a little while longer. He was so much fun to look at and listen to. She had to keep touching the ring on her finger to assure herself that their engagement wasn't a figment of her imagination.

"Go home and sleep for a few hours," he suggested. "Then call me the minute you wake up, and we'll spend the evening together."

"Okay." She yawned. "Too bad you have to work tomorrow."

He fed her some more guacamole. "Too bad *you* have to work tomorrow night. I won't see you until Tuesday night."

"No, I'm working Tuesday night, too. But I'm off Wednesday."

"I'll be in Amarillo on business," Jake said morosely. "I won't be back until late Thursday. When you will be…"

"Working," she said on a sigh.

"This is ridiculous." Jake dragged another chip through the salsa. "When I was killing myself trying to avoid you, you were showing up everywhere. Now I can't even plan a date with you." Apparently too disgruntled to eat the chip, he dropped it on his plate.

"I'll be back on days next week," Maddie said. "We can have some real dates then."

"Anything you want." With his fork, Jake speared a strip of bell pepper and a small piece of steak from his fajita and held it to her mouth. "But as soon as we get some lunch in you, you're going home to sleep for a while."

Maddie had feared she would be too excited to sleep, but when she finally tore herself away from Jake and went home, she was out the instant her head touched her pillow. She slept for five solid hours, then called Jake and arranged to meet him at his place.

They sipped iced tea and talked for a few minutes, then decided to go for a drive. The evening was growing cool, and Maddie was wearing only a T-shirt with her jeans, so Jake disappeared into his bedroom and emerged a minute later carrying two Texas Longhorns sweatshirts, one of which he tossed to Maddie.

She pretended disappointment as she watched him tug his sweatshirt over his head. "You don't have anything in yellow?"

A smile jerked at the corner of his mouth. "Sorry, honey, but they don't come in yellow. Burnt orange is your new favorite color, okay?"

"Hmm." She pushed her arms into the sleeves. "I guess if I'm going to be your woman, I should wear your colors."

She loved the grin he gave her in response.

They went for a short drive in the hills, stopped at Jimmy's Drive-In for cheeseburgers and ended up at the park on the river just as the sun was beginning to set.

"Did you call your mother?" Jake asked as he pulled Maddie down beside him on the bench where she'd first kissed him.

"Not yet. You know I love Mama, but she'll be so excited about me getting married that I won't get her off the phone for an hour." And she hadn't wanted to be away from Jake even one minute longer than she had to. This was still too new. She couldn't believe Jake wanted to marry her, and she couldn't get enough of gazing into his eyes, listening to his voice, holding his hand.

And kissing him. Her man had a phenomenal talent for kissing.

She finger-combed his hair. "I'll call her late tonight or in the morning. "She'll be thrilled when she hears I'm going to marry you."

Jake played with the fingers of her other hand, which he held in both of his. "Are you sure this isn't moving too fast for you? I don't need any time, but if you do, Maddie, you can have it. As much as you want."

"I'm not ready to set a date yet," she said slowly. "Not because I'm not sure, but because of…"

"Whitney," he finished for her.

She nodded. "Jake, I know she might be…" For the first time, Maddie made herself say the word. "She might be dead. It's been two months, and there's been no trace of her or John. But I can't help thinking there's still a small chance. And I'd hate for her to come home and find out that she'd missed helping Mama and me with all the wedding plans."

"So we'll wait." Jake lifted his arm over her head and snuggled her closer to his side.

"Thanks for understanding." Maddie twisted her neck to gaze up into his face. "I know you don't think they'll come home. But—"

"Actually, I've changed my mind about that."

"Changed your mind?"

He caught her chin in his hand. "I believe it's possible that they'll come home. Granted, I didn't believe that until a few hours ago, but I believe it now."

"What changed your mind?"

"The Lord did. I've almost lost count of all the amazing things He's done for me, for *us,* since I got out of bed this morning. I didn't think any of this was possible, but it happened. So now I'm wide open to other possibilities. I'm finished putting limits on what I believe God can do. Anything can happen, Maddie. And that has to mean it's never wrong to hope."

She stared into his marvelous dark eyes. There were still plenty of mysteries there, and it would be her privilege to spend the rest of her life unraveling them one by one. "I tried to stop hoping about *you,*" she said. "I told myself it was no use. Even if you were a little in love with me, you'd never admit it. But I couldn't stop hoping. I guess that's just my nature."

"That's what terrified me," he said. "Every time I ran into you, your sweet, sunny spirit eroded more of my bitterness. I realize now that I clung so tightly to my anger because I thought that was where my strength came from." He shook his head. "It's amazing how twisted your thoughts can become when you wander away from God."

Jake had told her everything that had happened at his mother's house, including the part where his mother had pulled off the diamond ring she'd worn for more than forty years and pressed it into Jake's hand. "'It's a flawless one-and-a-half-carat stone,'" she'd said, "'but more important than that, it was given to me by the only man I ever loved.'"

Jake had worried that Maddie might prefer to pick out her own engagement ring. But how could she not love this ring, which had come to her with such a beautiful history? It was a little loose on her finger, so she'd have to give it up long enough to have it resized. But it was *her* ring now. At least, it would be hers until the day she handed it over to one of Jake's sons.

"I can't wait to show Mama this ring," she said, twitching her fingers and watching the diamond shoot multicolored sparks.

"I just hope she's not too shocked by the suddenness of all this," Jake said. "I mean, we haven't even been dating."

Maddie thought about that. "You know, somehow I don't think she'll be at all surprised."

"*My* mama sure wasn't. It was like she saw this coming.

I'd told her you were in Prairie Springs, but I don't remember saying anything more than that." He looked at the river. "But I must have, because she knew."

Maddie thought back to her own mother's odd comments about Jake. She'd known things that Maddie was certain she'd never told her. It was almost as if…

Yes, that had to be it.

"Jake, has your mother mentioned my mother recently?"

He frowned. "No. They lost touch years ago. Didn't they?"

"*Did* they?"

Jake tipped his head back and narrowed his eyes, speculating. "You don't think they—"

"What other explanation is there? Jake, our mamas have been talking."

They stared at each other for a moment and then burst out laughing.

"Oh, *look,*" Maddie breathed, having just caught sight of the most beautiful sunset she'd seen in years. Over the vibrant orange-red disc of the sun, the sky was streaked with reds and oranges and pinks. "That looks like you could walk on it," she said, pointing to where the sun's reflection painted a shimmering orange-gold path across the water.

"Pretty." Jake sounded almost bored. "But I've seen even prettier things than that." He tugged meaningfully on a lock of her hair.

She smiled, then thought of her mother again. "Jake, should we tell our mamas we figured out their secret?"

"Nah. Let them have their fun." He kissed the tip of her nose. "And we'll have ours." He kissed her again, on the mouth this time, and then leaned his head against the top of hers. "Maddie, do you have any idea how much I loved flying helicopters?"

"I have some idea." Her heart ached for him. He would never again fly a helicopter, but she intended to do everything in her power to help make his life satisfying in other ways.

He captured a lock of her hair and twisted it around his finger. "For the last few years, I've thought the rest of my life could never be as exciting as the first part was. But you mentioned Job earlier, and I was just thinking about him. God allowed him to lose almost everything—but what happened in the end?"

Maddie wasn't sure what he was getting at, but she answered, "The Bible says the Lord blessed the last part of Job's life even more than the first."

"That's right. Not that I compare myself to Job—he was blameless and I'm as big a sinner as there ever was. It's just that when God took flying away from me, I thought the best part of my life was over. Then today He gave me a fresh start and He gave me you. And *today* has been the best day of my life."

"For me, too," she whispered.

Jake kissed her again, then he sighed deeply and looked across the river at the red-streaked sky over Fort Bonnell. "I've never been so excited in my life," he said. "I can't wait to see what the Lord has in store for us."

* * * * *

Be sure to read the next heartwarming installment in Homecoming Heroes, *A MATTER OF THE HEART, by Patricia Davids. Available October 2008 from Steeple Hill Love Inspired.*

Dear Reader,

In this story, Jake Hopkins has suffered both extreme physical pain and severe mental anguish. In his despair, he has turned away from God, but the steadfast love and faithful prayers of Maddie Bright help him find his way home. After Jake reconciles with God, his healing begins and his eyes are opened to a world of exciting possibilities.

If you are in a dark place right now, hiding from God, I urge you to give yourself up. You will never find contentment anywhere else. And if your heart is breaking because a loved one does not know or has wandered away from the Lord, just keep praying. You never know how or when God will answer.

Thank you for reading AT HIS COMMAND. If the story touched your heart, I'd be deeply grateful if you'd share it with your friends. Then maybe you'd like to drop by my Web site, BrendaCoulter.com, or shoot an e-mail, which I will answer personally, to Mail@BrendaCoulter.com.

Trusting Him,

Brenda Coulter

QUESTIONS FOR DISCUSSION

1. Maddie believes she doesn't have what it takes to be a hero. Jake disagrees. List some of the heroic qualities he sees in her.

2. Discuss when and how Jake's brotherly affection for Maddie begins to change into romantic love.

3. Why do you think the author chose Psalm 30:11-12 as the theme verse for this story? Can you think of some other verses that would be appropriate?

4. When he urged her to "keep Mama cheered up," Noah unwittingly placed a heavy burden on his sister's shoulders. Do you think Maddie's experience in the Middle East would have been different had she realized earlier that it wasn't her job to make everybody happy?

5. What scene in this book strikes you as the most romantic, and why?

6. List some of the things you believe might have fuelled Maddie's childhood crush on Jake. Compare those to the qualities she sees and admires in him after they meet again in Prairie Springs.

7. Estranged from God, Jake doesn't pray or attend church. Yet he gives generously of his time to a Christian

charity, Children of the Day. Why do you think he chose to support that particular organization?

8. Choose two or three minor characters from this story and discuss how they influenced Maddie's and/or Jake's actions and attitudes.

9. Jake chose to live and work next to the army base where he had trained as an Apache pilot, yet he never allowed himself to look at or even think about helicopters. Why do you think he settled in Prairie Springs?

10. Until the end of this story, Jake believes his actions resulted in Noah's death. Maddie maintains that Noah's time on earth was up, and that God would have taken him one way or another. What do you think it means when God takes our loved ones "before their time?"

11. Maddie is eager to buy a house and make Prairie Springs her permanent home. What do you think draws her so strongly to the town and the people?

12. No longer able to fly helicopters, Jake was convinced he'd never be happy again. Discuss how his reconciliation with God freed him to love Maddie and filled him with hope and excitement about the future.

13. While reading or after finishing this book, were you moved to ponder any spiritual truths? If so, what were they?

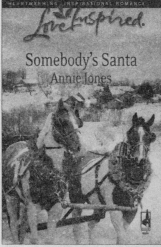

Love Inspired.
HISTORICAL

INSPIRATIONAL HISTORICAL ROMANCE

Years after being wrenched from Alice Shepard's life due to his lowborn status, Nicholas Tennant returns to London. Now wealthy and influential, he seeks revenge on Alice and her family. Alice is now a beautiful, grown woman and a loving single mother, and Nicholas cannot deny his feelings for her. Can he abandon his thirst for revenge and become the man most worthy of her love?

Look for

A Man Most Worthy

by

RUTH AXTELL MORREN

Available October wherever books are sold.

www.SteepleHill.com

Steeple Hill®

LIH82797

REQUEST YOUR FREE BOOKS!

2 FREE INSPIRATIONAL NOVELS
PLUS 2
FREE
MYSTERY GIFTS

YES! Please send me 2 FREE Love Inspired® novels and my 2 FREE mystery gifts (gifts are worth about $10). After receiving them, if I don't wish to receive any more books, I can return the shipping statement marked "cancel". If I don't cancel, I will receive 4 brand-new novels every month and be billed just $4.24 per book in the U.S. or $4.74 per book in Canada, plus 25¢ shipping and handling per book and applicable taxes, if any*. That's a savings of over 20% off the cover price! I understand that accepting the 2 free books and gifts places me under no obligation to buy anything. I can always return a shipment and cancel at any time. Even if I never buy another book, the two free books and gifts are mine to keep forever.

113 IDN ERXA 313 IDN ERWX

Name	(PLEASE PRINT)	
Address		Apt. #
City	State/Prov.	Zip/Postal Code

Signature (if under 18, a parent or guardian must sign)

Order online at www.LoveInspiredBooks.com

Or mail to Steeple Hill Reader Service:

IN U.S.A.: P.O. Box 1867, Buffalo, NY 14240-1867
IN CANADA: P.O. Box 609, Fort Erie, Ontario L2A 5X3

Not valid to current subscribers of Love Inspired books.

Want to try two free books from another series?
Call 1-800-873-8635 or visit www.morefreebooks.com

* Terms and prices subject to change without notice. N.Y. residents add applicable sales tax. Canadian residents will be charged applicable provincial taxes and GST. Offer not valid in Quebec. This offer is limited to one order per household. All orders subject to approval. Credit or debit balances in a customer's account(s) may be offset by any other outstanding balance owed by or to the customer. Please allow 4 to 6 weeks for delivery. Offer available while quantities last.

Your Privacy: Steeple Hill Books is committed to protecting your privacy. Our Privacy Policy is available online at www.SteepleHill.com or upon request from the Reader Service. From time to time we make our lists of customers available to reputable third parties who may have a product or service of interest to you. If you would prefer we not share your name and address, please check here. ☐

LIREG08R

Love Inspired®

TITLES AVAILABLE NEXT MONTH

Don't miss these four stories in October

SOMEBODY'S SANTA by Annie Jones

His mother's dying wish has brought Burke Burdett back into
Dora Hoag's life. Together they have a chance to play secret Santa
for the less fortunate…and perhaps a second chance at the love
Dora thought she'd lost forever.

A MATTER OF THE HEART by Patricia Davids
Homecoming Heroes

Dr. Nora Blake's job is to save lives, not talk to handsome
reporters. But Robert Dale does seem to care for Nora and her
patients. Will his talent for getting the story be enough to win
him Nora's heart?

SNOWBOUND IN DRY CREEK by Janet Tronstad
Dry Creek

Rodeo champion Zach Lucas got more than he bargained for
when he agreed to play Santa and deliver gifts to widowed
mother Jenny Collins. Especially when he found himself snowed
in on Christmas Eve with a beautiful woman and a little girl who
needed help finding the true meaning of Christmas.

HIS LITTLE COWGIRL by Brenda Minton

Six years ago, Cody Jacobs left the woman he loved without
a second thought. Now a new Christian, he's come to make
amends—only to meet the daughter he never knew existed.
Cody struggles to become a part of the family he didn't know
he had. But Bailey Cross may not be willing to trust him with
their daughter's heart…or her own.

LICNM0908